CHRISTMAS TALES

CHRISTMAS TALES

JOHN B. KEANE

MERCIER PRESS

Mercier Press
PO Box 5, 5 French Church Street, Cork
24 Lower Abbey Street, Dublin 1

© John B. Keane 1993

ISBN 1 85635 061 4

A CIP is available for this book from the British Library.

TO MARIE WITH LOVE

Printed in Ireland by Colour Books Ltd.

CONTENTS

Twelve Days' Grace

AGNES MALLOWAN SHOT the iron bolts into place in the back and front doors of the presbytery. Then she did the rounds of the house upstairs and downstairs, securing the windows in the curate's room but firmly resisting the temptation to inspect his belongings. She could have carried out the inspection with impunity if she so wished, she told herself, seeing that he was enjoying a short Christmas break at the other end of the diocese in his parents' home.

As was his wont the parish priest Father Canty would read in bed until she brought him his nightcap after which he would fall fast asleep until the seven o'clock bell sounded.

There had been no exchange of Christmas presents. As always he had handed her an extra week's pay but repeated his insistence that she was not to invest in a present on his behalf. From the beginning he had made it clear that there were to be no Christmas gifts.

'The best present you can give me,' he had warned, 'is to keep your money in your purse.'

Neither would he let her spoil him. 'Plain fare for me,' he would raise his hand aloft, 'and the plainer the better.'

The few luxuries he permitted himself were the nocturnal glass of punch and a glass of wine on Sundays with his dinner. He had partaken of wine earlier that day but only, he had reminded her, because it was Christmas. Sometimes she worried about his health. What concerned her most was the wheezing when he paused on the landing, having forgotten to take his time when ascending the stairs. She used every conceivable subterfuge lest he over-exert himself.

Sometimes his irritability showed when he found the cob tackled and waiting preparatory to a sick call.

'Who tackled the cob?' he would ask pretending to be angrier than he really was. There would be no answer while she prepared him for the journey. There were times, he would reluctantly admit to himself, during epidemics as the calls came pouring in when he was grateful. Normally the chores of catching and tackling the cob would fall to the sacristan but such a post had been vacant for years.

'The parish just can't afford it,' he had explained only the year before to the bishop who had intimated in his usual roundabout way that the elderly parish priest ought to be taking things easier.

'I'm only seventy-three,' Father Canty had retorted mischievously, 'which makes me two years younger than my bishop.'

'True,' came the unruffled response, 'but I don't have to go on sick calls at all hours of the night and you do and that is why I am giving you a curate. You have been playing on my conscience a lot lately.'

'We can't afford a curate,' Father Canty responded testily.

'We'll manage,' the bishop had concluded blithely.

The curate, Father Scanlan, had proved himself to be a hardworking, likeable young man well able to generate income through football tournaments, carddrives, raffles and silver circles. The parishioners might protest about the cost but they quickly became involved in the new activities and were to wonder in the course of time how they had managed to retain their sanity for so long without such diversions. Unfortunately for him Agnes Mallowan saw the new addition as an interloper whose every act seemed calculated to usurp the authority of the ageing parish priest. She felt it her duty to protect her employer. The younger man sensed her hostility but was prepared for it and had been counselled by colleagues in the art of countering it.

8

'Play second fiddle to the parish priest,' he was advised, 'and she won't see you as a threat to him.'

In truth, the new curate presented a greater threat to the housekeeper. She knew this from the beginning. When Father Canty retired and retire he must, sooner rather than later, she would find herself unemployed. There would be no place for her in the Old Priests' Home where elderly parish priests spent their declining years. No lay people were employed on the staff which was made up exclusively of nuns. With care, however, and unremitting attention to Father Canty's welfare she would see to it that it would be many a year before he relinquished his pastorship. Please God they would sustain each other to the very end. It would not be her fault if his parochial duties were terminated prematurely.

Agnes Mallowan heaved a great sigh of contentment as she poured the boiling water over the whiskey, lemon, sugar and cloves in the tall glass. The sugar began to melt instantly while the glistening lemon surfaced tantalisingly at the rim.

Agnes Mallowan inhaled the uprising steam and wondered, not for the first time, if she was placing her Confirmation pledge in jeopardy. Always she would reassure herself that there was no harm in steam and that the whiskey content therein was at such a minimum that it must surely be rendered ineffective before infiltrating the nostrils.

Just to be sure that her pledge remained intact she inhaled only once. She might have averted her head but then how would she identify the tiny foreign bodies such as flecks, specks and motes which needed to be extracted from his reverence's punch before she deemed it worthy for delivery not that he would notice for he always kept his eyes firmly closed as he swallowed.

He drank noisily.

'There is no satisfaction,' he would explain, 'unless I can hear myself drinking. It helps me relish the punch even more.'

From the moment he closed his eyes preparatory to the first swallow he would keep them closed, blindly extending the glass in her general direction, before drawing the coverlet under his chin. She always stood in close attendance while he drank and, upon receipt of the glass, would lower the wick in the shapely globe of the paraffin lamp before blowing out the flame. Then she would withdraw silently, closing the bedroom door behind her. Now, as she gently stirred the amber mixture with a slender spoon before embarking on the upstairs journey, the contentment departed her placid features and was replaced by a frown. It was a frown with which every parishioner in the remote, rambling parish was familiar. Agnes Mallowan was best avoided while the frown was in residence. Otherwise she was good-humoured and tractable. The frown deepened when the front door bell rang for the second time.

'Let them wait!' she spoke out loud and ascended the tarpaulin covered stairs. Gently she knocked on the bedroom door.

'Come!' the response was immediate.

She stood silently at the bedside while he closed the leather-bound copy of *Ivanhoe* without marking the page and placed it on the table near the bed. He liked to open the covers of his favourite novels at random and proceed from the beginning of the paragraph which presented itself.

'It was a quiet Christmas thank God,' he said as he accepted the punch. He swallowed without closing his eyes and she knew that he had heard the front door bell. He would ask about it. If only she had brought him the punch ten minutes earlier he would be fast asleep and the caller or callers could be fobbed off till morning.

Certain parishioners, especially the more isolated, had a habit of making mountains out of molehills as far as sick calls were concerned.

'Better go and see who's at the door Agnes,' he spoke resignedly, 'we don't want to be the cause of

10

sending some poor soul to hell for the want of a priest.'

'Yes Father. At once Father,' she answered dutifully. She could truthfully say that never once had she questioned one of his commands in all of her twenty years as his housekeeper. He was a good man. Others had not been so good, other employers after her husband had expired prematurely and left her with four young children, all now safely emigrated to America and corresponding regularly. Her husband had not been a good man nor had her father. Her two brothers had been good men. She remembered them fondly. No need to pray for them. She knew for sure they went straight to heaven when they died. She prayed every night for her husband and her father. God knows they needed prayers if ever a pair needed them.

In the doorway she addressed herself to the two men who stood together sheepishly, one waiting for the other to open the negotiations.

'Where did ye get the rain?' she asked coldly, 'there's nothing but a bare mist outside.'

'That's the thick mist up the mountain missus,' the taller of the pair informed her.

She looked from one to the other without inviting them in. They wore tattered overcoats but no headgear. The rain had plastered their scant grey hair to their heads.

'How did ye come?' Agnes Mallowan asked.

'We walked missus,' from the smaller man.

Agnes recognised him from the way he shuffled his feet. He indulged in the same motions when he stood outside the church on Sundays. From the age of fourteen onwards neither had entered the parish church. They came to church all right but only to stand with their backs to the outside walls while the Mass was in progress. She would attest under oath that they never paid Christmas dues nor oats' money nor any church offerings so that their priest could keep body and soul together and feed and pay his housekeeper and curate. Now, more than likely, they would have somebody

11

sick, so sick, or so they believed, that a priest was required. Her worst fears were realised when the taller asked if the curate was available.

'You know as well as I do that he's gone home for Christmas and won't be back until the day after tomorrow. In fact the whole parish knows it.'

'Well then,' from the smaller brother, 'himself will have to do. Our dada is dying and he needs a priest.'

'And who decided your dada was dying?'

'Doctor,' the taller responded smugly.

'And when did he have the doctor?' Agnes, a veteran of rustic interrogation, wasn't going to allow the parish priest out on such a night till she had confirmed that death was imminent.

'Two hours ago,' came the reply.

'And why didn't the doctor get in touch with us?' she asked.

''Cos,' said the other brother, 'him be gone to the other side of the mountain to deliver a baby and there's rumours of a man killed when his horse and cart capsized farther on. There's other calls too.'

'Ye can bide yeer time out in one of the sheds for a while then,' the housekeeper informed them, 'till 'tis a bit closer to morning. Father Canty needs a few hours sleep.'

'Our dada won't last that long,' the taller brother placed a leg in the hallway. 'Him was gasping and us leaving,' the smaller added, pushing the taller man forward.

'Mind don't ye wet my hallway that I polished specially for Christmas,' Agnes Mallowan countered as she pushed the persistent pair to the outside.

'Call the priest before we call him!' the tone of the taller brother's voice was unmistakably threatening.

'Who is it Agnes?' Father Canty called from the upstairs landing.

'The Maldooney brothers looking for a priest Father.'

'The Maldooneys of Farrangarry is it?' Father Canty

12

asked.

'None other,' Agnes threw a withering look at the unwelcome visitors.

'Ask them in for God's sake. I'll go tackle the cob.'

'Let one of these tackle him,' Agnes called back as she withdrew to allow them access to the kitchen where the parish priest joined them.

'No,' he spoke half to himself as he took stock of the dripping brothers, 'make them a pot of tea. I'll see to the cob. Light a lantern while you're at it Agnes.'

Obedient to a fault the cob, stout, firm and round, submitted itself to harness and backed itself docilely between the long slender shafts. Father Canty draped a partially filled oats' bag around the powerful crest and returned to the kitchen.

The brothers sat amazed as the housekeeper prepared the parish priest for his journey. They were even more amazed when, childlike, he submitted himself to her fussy ministrations which began with the removal of his slippers and their replacement with stout, strong boots and gaiters. She then removed the short coat which he had worn to the stable and placed a heavy woollen scarf around his neck and shoulders. This was followed by a heavy woollen cardigan and a heavier short coat and finally on top of all came a long leather coat which reached all the way down to his ankles. With mouths open the brothers watched in wonder as she placed a wide-rimmed black hat on his balding pate and, finally, handed him the small suitcase which contained the oils, missal and stole. All that remained to be done was the collecting of the sacred host from the tabernacle and here, they were surprised to note, the housekeeper had no role.

'You'll find dry sacks in there,' Father Canty indicated an outhouse. 'They'll cover your heads and shoulders.'

They were surprised when he opened the trap door for them. They would not have been dismayed if they had been called upon to walk behind. After three miles

13

of moderately undulating ground they entered the side road which would take them to the Maldooney abode, three-quarters of the way up the mountain. It was a steep climb but not for a single moment did it tax the short-gaited cob. After the first mile when they left the presbytery there was no attempt at conversation. Despite repeated attempts to involve them Father Canty gave up. He found it difficult to stay awake without the stimulus of verbal conversation. He attempted a rosary but there were no responses forthcoming. Thereafter, he prayed silently to himself. He was not unduly worried. The cob had conveyed him safely in the past while he slept and could be depended upon to do so again. When eventually they reached the Maldooney abode some waiting neighbours came forward and took charge of the cob.

The old man lay propped on an ancient iron bed. His breathing was erratic but his eyes opened when he beheld the priest in the faint light of the three spluttering candles, precariously placed especially for the occasion on the mantelpiece, bedpost and window sill.

'You'll hear my last confession Father?'

Father Canty was surprised. The voice was weak and spluttering like the candles but there seemed to be no doubt that he was strong enough to make himself understood.

Two elderly women, shawled and praying, vacated the room the moment the priest bent his head to hear the sins of the dying penitent. The old man went on and on sometimes incoherently but mostly articulate as he recited the sins of a lifetime. He was well prepared for the ultimate shriving. He did not spare himself as the nauseating recall of human folly poured forth. Then suddenly he stopped, gasped and fell into a deep sleep from which, all present were agreed, he would never wake.

The ritual over, Father Canty left the house and entered his transport but not before he turned the bottom and dry side of the trap cushion upward. There was no sign of the brothers. The neighbours could not explain it. One minute they were in the kitchen standing with their backs to the dying fire and the next they were nowhere to be seen.

Agnes Mallowan was on her feet the moment she heard the hoof-beats at the rear of the presbytery. When she drew the bolt and went outside the animal was standing still. In the trap Father Canty was fast asleep, the rain dripping from his hat. Gently she awakened him and led him indoors. She seated him close to the fire where she had drawn the kitchen table.

'You're a lifesaver Agnes,' he spoke with unconcealed fervency as he ravenously spooned the steaming giblet soup into his waiting mouth. She tip-toed from the kitchen and up the stairs. She lit the paraffin lamp and replaced the hot water bottle with another of more immediate vintage. As she silently descended the stairs she met him on his way up. He seemed to be overcome by drowsiness. She allowed a short interval to pass before knocking at the bedroom door.

'Come,' came the voice.

'You have it well-earned,' she assured him when he expressed doubt about his entitlement to the extra punch. She stood by while he swallowed and took the empty glass when it was extended to her. She quenched the lamp and closed the bedroom door behind her. Rarely did he snore but he snored now. The snores were long and profound. As she passed his bedroom door a short while later the snores were deep and even. She could not believe her ears when the irritating sound of the front door bell shattered the silence.

'What now?' she asked as she hurried down the stairs lest the continuous tinkling disturb her master's slumber.

'Who's out in God's name?' she called without drawing the bolt.

'It's us missus,' came the unmistakable voice of the taller Maldooney.

15

Slowly Agnes Mallowan drew the bolt and opened the door.

They stood huddled together as they did on the previous visit. Agnes Mallowan folded her arms and spread her legs across the width of the doorway to prevent access to the hallway. The brothers, dripping wet, looked at each other and then at the housekeeper.

'State your business,' she said coldly.

'We want the priest,' from the taller brother.

'Is it to pay him the Christmas dues you want him?' Agnes asked as the smaller of the pair snuffled and sniffled, sensing that there was to be no tea on this occasion.

'We want the priest for our father,' he explained between sniffles, 'he forgot a sin. '

'And you expect Father Canty to get out of his bed and go back up the mountain to Farrangarry because your dada forgot to tell him he wet the bed.'

'Oh now!' said the smaller brother, ''tis a deal worse than wetting the bed. No one will go to hell for wetting the bed but fornicating will get you there on the double.'

'Fornicating!' the housekeeper's curiosity got the better of her.

'And who was he fornicating with?' she asked.

'Never mind who,' from the taller brother. 'It's enough for you to know that he'll face the fires of hell on account of he deliberately failing to mention this particular one.'

Agnes Mallowan found herself in a dilemma. If she called Father Canty the journey to Farrangarry and back could be the death of him. If she didn't call him and the man died with an unforgiven sin on his soul she would be guilty of sending a soul to hell. She came down in favour of her employer.

'I'm not calling him,' she said, and was about to close the door when the smaller man pushed her backwards into the hallway.

'You call him,' he shouted angrily.

16

Agnes Mallowan stood her ground. Her mission in life was to protect her master. She decided on a change of tack.

'There's no fear of your dada,' she assured them.

'Without a priest he's bound for hell,' the taller brother pushed the smaller forward.

The housekeeper refused to be intimidated. Not an inch of ground did she yield.

'Didn't I tell ye there was no fear of him,' she drew herself upwards and re-folded her arms, 'for don't it say in the Cathecism that hell is closed for the twelve days of Christmas and anyone who dies during that period goes direct to heaven.'

The brothers exchanged dubious glances.

''Tis there in black and white,' the housekeeper assured them.

The brothers turned their backs on her and consulted in whispers. After several moments they faced her secondly.

'You're sure?' the smaller asked.

'Why would I say it if it was a lie?' she countered.

'Why then,' the taller brother asked, 'did the priest come all the way up to the mountain if there was no hell?'

'Mohammed went to the mountain didn't he?' Agnes replied with a straight face, 'and there was no hell.'

Both brothers shuffled uneasily at this revelation. Comment proved to be beyond them. What she said was irrefutable. Also was she not well placed to be in the know about such matters. She was of the presbytery, therefore, of the church and of the inner circle at that. The Catechism had always confounded the Maldooney brothers in their schooldays and this woman was confounding them now.

'Go on away home,' she said, 'and let yeer minds be at ease. If yeer dada is dead his soul is in heaven and if he's not dead it will be there soon. '

Slowly, sheepishly the brothers backed away from

the door. Exhausted she shot the bolts and retired upstairs to the sleep of the just. On the Sunday after
Christmas she was delighted to see the brothers in
their customary positions outside the church as the
holy Mass proceeded solemnly within. Sidling up to
the smaller of the pair she enquired in a whisper after
his father.

'He's sitting up,' came the happy response.

'He's eating a bite,' the taller brother concurred.

'Well I declare,' Agnes Mallowan joined her hands
together as though she were about to pray.

The smaller brother cleared his throat and permitted himself a toothless smile as he disclosed in rever-
ential whispers, out of respect to his surroundings,
that the quickly recovering parent intended presenting
himself at Cassidy's wren-dance on the following Sat-
urday night, a mere six days away. Agnes made a
mental note to enquire from one of her many parochial
informants about the general goings-on at Cassidy's
wren-dance and about the antics of Maldooney senior
in particular.

She admitted her source by the rear door of the
presbytery one week later. Maldooney senior had ex-
celled himself, displaying a variety of fancy steps that
put younger terpsichoreans to shame. He crowned his
display by dancing a hornpipe at the request of a bux-
om lady from the other end of the parish and astound-
ed all and sundry by enticing her to the well-filled hay
shed at the bottom of Cassidy's haggard where they
sojourned rapturously till the dawn's early light reminded them that it was time to go their separate
ways. They promised to meet again while the sons, for
better or for worse, did nothing but stand idly by and
never once opened their porter-stained mouths to any
member of the opposite sex.

A CHRISTMAS VISITOR

THE UNIQUE SET of circumstances which preceded the arrival of John J. Mulholland merchant tailor into the world deserve to be recorded, at least according to John J. Mulholland.

'I will,' he declared as we sat in Mikey Joe's Irish-American bar in the seaside resort of Ballybunion, 'offer up a novena of rosaries for your intentions provided you adorn futurity with my peculiar beginnings.'

John J. was never direct when he could be diffuse.

'My paternal grandfather,' he began before I could drain my glass and make good my escape, 'hated Christmas and if he could lay his hands on Santa Claus he would surely dismember him. He used to stuff his ears with cotton wool to shut out the sound of Christmas bells and usen't he disappear altogether on Christmas Eve, moving off with a day's provisions at first light and not returning until long after dark.'

'It's your face that attracts them,' a boozing companion had observed earlier in the day when a man I had never seen before shot from a shop door and seized me by both wrists. He was a powerfully built fellow but, alas, a victim of the most excruciating halitosis. He held me fast for several minutes while he recalled the treachery of the wife who had abandoned him without warning for an amorous greengrocer.

John J. Mulholland did not hold me by the wrists but his ample frame overflowed a bar stool between myself and the exit. He was pointing at his neck around which was a crimson weal which might well have been caused by a hangman's rope.

'It's not what you're thinking,' he smiled grimly, 'and if you are patient you shall discover how it came to be where it is.'

I indicated to Mikey Joe that I wanted another whiskey. If I was going to suffer I would do so in comfort. My nemesis had also brought his stool nearer, totally eliminating every means of escape. The whole business had begun with the aforementioned paternal grandfather, one Jacko Mulholland, a trousers' maker with a tooth for whiskey and a profound hatred of Christmas.

When our tale begins Jacko was a mere thirty years of age. Both parents had died young and from the age of sixteen onwards he was left to fend for himself. Neighbours would explain in their good-natured neighbourly way that a general resentment for all things tender and sentimental had set in shortly after the demise of his father and mother.

'Say nothing to him about Christmas,' they would advise strangers who had no way of knowing about his bereavement, 'and whatever you do, do not wish him the compliments of the season.'

As is the way with neighbours they were patient with him when he reacted viciously to the least mention of the Yuletide season. They told themselves that his grief would diminish with the passage of time and would regularly trot out the old adages; time is a great healer and the years cure everything and so forth and so on but they were disappointed when, after fourteen of those very same years, he persisted in ignoring the arrival of Christmas.

His kitchen window sills and his mantelpiece were bare. None of the accumulation of Christmas cards so evident in the houses of his neighbours were to be seen in the Mulholland home. When a card arrived from a friend or relative he immediately consigned it to flame in the Stanley number eight.

'How dare they!' he would mutter to himself before returning to the stitching of the rough and ready trousers in which he specialised. Sometimes he thought of Mary Moles who lived just down the street and who was still unattached although she need not be for she was a trim cut of a girl with pleasant features and a virtuous name. She could have been his. All he had to do was ask. It had been understood. Their names had been linked since he started to pay her court but she grew tired of his moods and his own attitude hardened the longer the rift between them lasted. She would not marry another and neither would he but they cherished each other no longer. Concerned neighbours shook their heads at the woeful waste of it all. The entire street felt the pain of it and the entire street prayed that it would come right in the end.

'They'll be too old soon,' one old woman said at which another and then many others nodded sagely and concurred. In time the situation came to be accepted and the affair became part of the history of the street.

At this stage in the proceedings John J. Mulholland excused himself on the grounds that he had to visit the toilet. I could have vacated the scene there and then but I was hooked as indeed was my genial friend Mikey Joe. We spoke in undertones lest our voices carry to the toilet. Mikey Joe confided that he had long believed, as I did, that the disfiguring weal around John J.'s neck was caused by a hangman's noose but now we both knew better and hoped to be enlightened as to the true origins of the unprepossessing blemish before we were much older.

When John J. returned he resumed his position on the stool, swallowed from his glass and cleared his throat. We presumed foolishly that the clearing was the prelude to the remaining disclosures but not a solitary word was forthcoming. It was as though he had suddenly taken a vow of silence. Mikey Joe was first to get the message.

'Finish that,' he indicated John J.'s almost empty glass. As soon as the refill was placed in his hand John J. cleared his throat a second time, sniffed the whiskey, frowned, pondered, approved and sipped. He proceeded with his tale.

Apparently his grandfather Jacko was not above taking a drink now and then in the privacy of his kitchen. He always drank alone. On the morning of Christmas Eve he betook himself to the woods which surrounded the town and did not return till dark. He took with him the usual provisions and spent the day observing coot and heron as well as mallard and diver. He would have fished had the season been open. He listened without appreciation to the wide variety of songbirds who poured forth their tiny hearts as though they knew of the great celebration that was at hand. When Jacko came to the river he sat on an oak stump and, not for the first time, considered the dismal solution the depths below offered. As always he dismissed the thought but he would have to admit that the temptation grew stronger as the years went by.

A shiver went through him when he imagined his lifeless body laid out on a slab in the local morgue where he had once seen the decaying remains of a boy who had accidentally drowned some years before.

'I haven't the courage.' He spoke the words out loud and no sooner had they departed his lips than a hunting stoat wriggled its way urgently upwards from a small declivity at his feet before disappearing into the undergrowth.

He rose quickly, his dreary reverie suspended yet again. Shortly afterwards dusk began to infiltrate the woodlands. The face of the river darkened. Overhead the stars began to twinkle. The moon brightened as the sun dipped beneath the tree-tops to the west. From the depths of the woods came the unmistakable sounds of rooting badgers, heedless now that the evening shadows were merging into one.

Jacko Mulholland gathered himself and followed the river bank towards the lights of the town. A bell rang sweetly, its sacred tones carrying far up the placid river. Jacko Mulholland thrust his fingers into his ears and stood stock still. He would wait until the infernal pealing came to an end.

As he left the wood and entered the town the dark in all its fullness had fallen. In the kitchen of his silent home he stoked the range fire which he had earlier packed carefully with wet turf sods as well as dry to ensure its survival until his return. He lit the paraffin lamp and looked at the calendar which hung nearby. He took a pencil from the window sill and crossed out the offending date, December twenty-fourth, nineteen twenty-two. A few days now and the whole fraud would be over, the entire shambles brushed aside to make way for the new year. He decided to postpone his supper till nearer bedtime. Anyway he had eaten his fill in the woodlands before the arrival of dusk. He added several small dry sods to the fire and sat in the ancient, walnut rocking-chair which had been in use since his great-grandfather's time and which was the nearest thing to a family heirloom one would find if one searched every house in the street.

There was a long night ahead. It would be the longest in the fourteen years since the disaster if normal progression was anything to go by. He rocked for a while in the vain hope that slumber would come. He knew in advance that it would be a futile bid. He rose and added some larger sods to the fire. Then from the recesses of the cupboard he withdrew a bottle of whiskey. He had purchased it in a nearby village after a football game to which he had cycled in late November with carrier bag attached for no other purpose. He shook the bottle thoroughly before uncorking. He stood it on the deal table for several minutes while he went in search of a glass. There was one somewhere, only one. He knew it wasn't in the cupboard. The people of the street kept their glasses, few as they were, in sideboards. Those who were not possessed of sideboards wrapped them carefully in old newspapers and arranged them loosely in a cardboard box which was always kept for safety under the parental bed.

He found himself searching the sideboard in the small sitting-room attached to the kitchen. Eventually he found the upturned glass under a tea cosy. He could not recall how it came to be there. He returned to the rocking-chair and stretched a hand as far as the whiskey bottle. He poured the contents into the four ounce glass until it was brimful. He sipped, spluttered and coughed. It was always like that, he recalled, with the first drop unless one was partial to whiskey diluted by water. In the street the menfolk never mixed spirits and water. When the whiskey was swallowed it was all right to swallow a mouthful of water after a decent interval but to mix it in the glass was regarded as far less edifying than the pure drop.

He placed the glass on the table next to the bottle and removed the mud-covered boots. He would clean them in the morning. Nobody could clean and polish boots like his late lamented mother. Nobody could untie lace knots like her. He used to call her his knot-ripper-in-chief. He recalled how his father had laughed loud and long when the title was first conferred. Ah those had been happy days!

The tears flowed down Jacko Mulholland's face, remembering his father and himself squatting on the workbench, his mother attentive and obedient to their wants. It was she who delivered the finished trousers when, for one reason or another, the customer failed to call. She never came back empty-handed. When she returned without the money she always brought the trousers home. She never extended credit. Sooner or later she would get her money. Alterations were child's play to her.

Jacko extended a hand for the bottle and refilled his glass. He could not bring himself to resurrect past Christmases. The memories were too painful. He found a block of cheddar in the cupboard and cut himself a slice. His thoughts turned to Mary Moles as they did at the same time every year. He wondered if he would be any happier if he had taken her for a wife. Too late now. He had seen the grey hairs on her head and the puckered face of her through his window as she passed up and down. Hers was a stately walk. She would have to be granted that. Never looking to left or right she moved with the grace of a swan. It was her natural gait. Everybody in the street would agree that she was one unflappable female, maybe a mite too steady and maybe a trifle too demure and maybe somewhat conservative but she was the kind of girl one could present anywhere. Certain people in other streets considered her dull but this assessment had to be based on ignorance. Her true worth was known only to her neighbours and they would swear in any court in the land that Mary Moles had a touch of class and they would also swear that class was what really mattered in the long run.

She lived with her father, a cantankerous old man, a martyr to lumbago and catarrh, who chided his only child day in day out. His wife, or so the neighbours maintained, had simply given up the ghost having been subjected to twenty years of withering criticism, all undeserved. The only respite she enjoyed was when she visited the church. Who could blame her if she spent as much time as possible in its hallowed precincts, kneeling and praying and savouring the blessed silence no end.

Jacko Mulholland surveyed the glowing fire. If it held together without collapsing it should last till bedtime. Next he surveyed the whiskey bottle and was pleased to see that more than half of its contents remained. There is nothing as consoling or sustaining to the half-drunken imbiber as the presence of a whiskey bottle more full than it is empty. It is as comforting as hidden battalions are to a field commander whose forces have been decimated by a succession of foolhardy charges. It is akin to the feelings of a man who, upon waking in the morning, expects to be confronted by rain and storm but instead finds the sun shining through his window.

Jacko Mulholland refilled his glass and swallowed copiously, gasping for breath as the amber liquid set

25

fire to his innards. Then he began to sob as he recalled other days – his mother's voice in the morning as she prepared breakfast, her gentle singing of the ancient songs, her lilting of dance tunes, hornpipe, jig and reel, her dulcet call from the foot of the stairs; fishing with his father and the delight when one or the other hooked a trout, sitting in the lamplight late at night watching his father tying flies. The sobbing became uncontrollable. Nobody heard for such was the extent of the celebrations in the neighbouring houses that no external sound had the power to penetrate the old stone walls. It was the same in every other house on the street save that of old Mick Moles and his daughter Mary. They sat silently at either side of the hearth. Sometimes he would call upon God to relieve his aches and other times he would call on the Blessed Virgin but if they heard they failed to bring him relief so that he rounded on his daughter before going to bed falsely accusing her of concocting watery tea and burning his toast.

Jacko Mulholland was now at that stage of drunkenness where the victim starts to natter to himself, grinding his teeth as he recalls all the injustices he has suffered since first entering the world. He turned his attention to the whiskey bottle and, blurred though his vision had become, he was sorry to note that more than two-thirds of its contents had been consumed. He mourned its passing with a series of deep sighs and tedious lamentations after which his head began to droop. Vainly he strove to restrain the slumber which seemed set to overpower him but he was a poor match for its stupefying subtlety. Soon he was snoring.

There are few snores with the depth and resonance of whiskey snores. They rebounded from the walls and filled the kitchen to overflowing. The only danger to the whiskey snorer is that, more often than not, his slumber is disrupted by one of his own creations. In this instance it was another sound which infiltrated Jacko Mulholland's malt-induced insensibility. At first he stirred irritably, grimaced and then groaned before opening bleary eyes. The first object to catch his eye was the mantelpiece clock. The hands indicated that he had slept for several hours. There was that annoying noise again. It sounded as if somebody was knocking at the front door but who could be knocking at twenty-past one in the morning? He decided to ignore it.

From time to time over the years he would be roused from his slumbers early on the mornings of religious festivals and football matches by agricultural labourers who would have specially commissioned new pairs of trousers for such occasions. He never minded, provided payment was forthcoming but this was different. Twenty minutes past one on the morning of Christmas was downright uncivil to say the least. He decided to ignore it, certain that the knocker would become discouraged after awhile. He reached out his hand for the whiskey bottle. This time he dispensed with the glass and lifted the jowl to his lips. The whiskey bubbled and gurgled as he upended the bottle. Just at that moment the knocking started again. He lowered the bottle and placed it on the table. The knocking persisted. He had never been subjected to anything quite like it and yet it wasn't loud nor was it sharp and still it grated to such a degree that he was obliged to place a finger in either ear. Normally this would succeed in at least diminishing the sound but not in this instance for the harder he pressed his fingers into the well-waxed canals the more piercing the knocking became. Perplexed he withdrew his fingers. Reluctantly he moved towards the door. He did not open it at once. He peered through the curtains of the sitting-room window in the hope of catching a glimpse of the knocker. There was nothing to be seen.

He climbed the stairs and entered the front bedroom. He looked down on to the street but there was nothing. Indeed, from his vantage point which afforded an unrestricted view of the entire street, there wasn't a solitary soul to be seen. All the sounds of revelry had long since abated and nothing stirred. The roadway was still wet after a heavy shower which had fallen while Jacko slept. A blissful calm had followed. Then came another bout of the nerve-shattering knocking. Silently he opened the window and, leaning out, peered downward. There was nothing. He withdrew but no sooner had he closed the window than the knocking commenced once more. He rushed down stairs and opened the door. Standing before him was a small boy who could not have exceeded seven or eight years in age. The youngster was impeccably dressed, shining white shoes, a snow-white shirt and red vermilion necktie, a double-breasted navy blue suit and a cream-coloured felt hat which he lifted respectfully from his immaculately slicked head as soon as Jacko Mulholland opened the door. On the child's face was an angelic smile. He was about to speak when Jacko seized him round the throat with his right thumb and index finger.

'Are you a lorgadawn or what!' Jacko roared as he tightened the grip on the pale, slender throat so easily encircled by the powerful fingers, stronger than any in the street from constant stitching, knotting and threading. The boy wriggled in his grasp, unable to answer.

'Are you a lorgadawn!' Jacko shouted a second time.

All the boy could do was shake his head but even this proved difficult. The pressure from the long, thin fingers was overpowering. Coarse and calloused they cut into his neck. Then, suddenly Jacko let go. The boy gingerly felt his throat where the fingers had lingered for so long.

'Who in God's name are you?' Jacko asked gruffly but with none of the fury which accompanied his first question.

'I'll tell you who I am if you promise to keep calm,' the boy replied.

'You have my promise,' came the assurance from Jacko.

'I am your grandson,' the boy informed him.

'My what?' Jacko roared.

'See,' said the boy, 'you're breaking your promise already. You promised you'd keep calm,' the boy replied.

'Is this some kind of joke boy?' Jacko asked fiercely and would have seized him again had not the visitor lifted his hand and announced solemnly that beyond any shadow of doubt he was indeed his grandson.

'But how can that be?' Jack asked. 'I am only thirty years of age and I was never married. In fact I was never with anyone but the one woman and I never put a hand above her knee.'

'The fact remains,' the boy was adamant, 'that I am your grandson John J. Mulholland.'

'I am also John J. Mulholland,' Jacko informed him, 'but they call me Jacko.'

'I should, of course, have said,' the visitor was apologetic now, 'that I will be your grandson in the course of time. Strictly speaking I am not your grandson right now. What you see before you is an unborn presence which will arrive into this world on a date yet to be decided.'

'Oh,' said Jacko Mulholland impressed by the boy's forthrightness, 'I see. I see. Would you like to step inside?'

'I cannot do that,' came the polite reply, 'but thank you all the same.'

Jacko suddenly knelt down and took the boy's hands gently in his.

'And to think,' he chided himself tearfully, 'I treated you so roughly and you my very own grandson, my flesh and blood.'

'Don't blame yourself,' young John J. Mulholland's tone held a wealth of tenderness, 'how could you know who I was until I told you.'

At this juncture he helped Jacko to his feet.

'There are certain conditions to be fulfilled,' he warned, 'before all this comes to pass.'

'I'll play my part,' Jacko spoke fervently, the tears coursing down his dishevelled face.

'Know one thing now for certain,' he said, 'and that is your grandfather won't be found wanting no matter what the score.'

'First you must marry,' young John J. insisted, 'and, which is more, if all the heavenly calculations are to be accurately realised, you will go to the altar with your bride in six months time to the very day.'

'My bride!' Jacko asked, 'who is she to be?'

'My grandmother, of course,' came the emphatic response.

'Yes. Yes,' Jacko entreated, 'but her name. Tell me her name.'

'Her name,' said young John J., 'is Mary Moles.'

'Yes. Yes,' Jacko promised slobberingly. 'I'll face her at first light and propose.'

'Now,' said young John J., 'I must leave you. I have a long journey and further delay could be fatal.'

'Will I see you again?' Jacko Mulholland asked plaintively.

'Of course you will,' came the positive response. 'You will teach me how to fish and how to tie flies like a true grandfather.'

'And,' Jacko paused before posing the next question, 'will I have much time with you?'

'Oh yes,' came the heart-lifting assurance, 'you will see me to the very threshold of manhood and when your job is done you will depart this worldly scene for the happier climes of heaven at the great age of eighty-four years. Now I must bid you farewell.'

So saying young John J. took his future grandfather's hand and kissed it gently. Then he was gone.

The street was empty but it was no longer desolate. Lights were coming on in the houses and there was the sound of a baby crying for its morning milk. There were other sounds, laughter and song snatches and the crowing of roosters and there were odours, the tantalising aroma of frying rashers, the age-old smell of turf and timber smoke and the salty tang of the distant sea in the rising breeze.

Like all lonely men Jacko Mulholland adored the morning. He regarded it as the fairest of all the day's times, unsullied and pure, ever adorning and gilding. A whistling milkman cycled past, his gallons rattling from either handle-bar.

'A happy Christmas to you Jacko,' he called and re-doubled his pedalling.

'And the same to you Eddie,' Jacko Mulholland shouted in his wake.

Later, after he had shaved and breakfasted, Jacko closed the front door behind him. The earliest of the Christmas morning Mass-goers were abroad, mostly elderly, fearful of being without a seat in the crowded church. Their reactions were mixed when Jacko, taciturn for fourteen years, extended the compliments of the season. Some responded instantly while others were so overcome by shock and surprise that words failed them.

'It's you is it?' Mary Moles valiantly strove to hide her surprise when she opened the door and saw him standing there. He followed her into the kitchen where her aged parent sat at the head of the table spooning porridge into a toothless mouth. Between spoonfuls he protested, in undertones, about the perfidy of humanity, indicting females in particular. His mouth opened wordlessly when he beheld Jacko Mulholland. It opened still wider when without warning of any kind Mary Moles found her upper body imprisoned in the arms of her one-time suitor. She protested not nor did she yield an inch of ground. Rather did she place her soft hands at the back of his neck and respond with all the vigour she could muster.

Six months later they were married and they lived happily ever after apart from a spirited row now and then which only served to enliven the relationship.

31

Thus ends John J. Mulholland's tale. It was told to him by his grandfather not long before the old man passed away at the ripe old age of eighty-four.

'As for me,' John Joe eased himself from his stool and handed his empty glass to Mikey Joe, 'I don't remember having hand, act or part in the proceedings.'

He moved to the life-sized mirror near the doorway, examined his reflection carefully and at length. He gingerly traced the finger-thin red weal, the origins of which, according to John J. Mulholland, had baffled the world's leading dermatologists since he was first referred to them by the family doctor at the tender age of eight!

THE *CURRICULUM VITAE*

FRED SPELLACY WOULD always remember the Christmas he spent as a pariah, not for the gloom and isolation it brought him nor for the abuse. He would remember it as a period of unprecedented decision-making which had improved his lot in the long term.

Fred Spellacy believed in Christmas. Man and boy it had fulfilled him and for this he was truly grateful. Of late his Christmases had been less happy but he would persevere with his belief, safe in the knowledge that Christmas would never really let him down.

'Auxiliary Postman Required'. The advertisement, not so prominently displayed on the window of the sub post office, captured Dolly Hallon's attention. Postmen are nice, Dolly thought and they're kind and, more importantly, everybody respects them. In her mind's eye she saw her father with his postbag slung behind him, his postman's cap tilted rakishly at the side of his head, a smile on his face as he saluted all and sundry on his way down the street.

If ever a postmaster, sub or otherwise, belied his imperious title that man was Fred Spellacy. It could be fairly said that he was the very essence of deferentiality. He was also an abuse-absorber. When things went wrong his superiors made him into a scapegoat, his customers rounded on him, his wife upbraided him, his in-laws chided him. His assistant Miss Finnerty clocked reproachfully as though she were a hen whose egg-laying had been precipitately disrupted. She reserved all her clocking for Fred. She never clocked at Fred's wife but then nobody did.

'Yes child!' Fred Spellacy asked gently.

'It's the postman's job sir.'

Fred Spellacy nodded, noted the pale, ingenuous face, the threadbare clothes.

'What age are you?' he asked gently.

'Eleven,' came the reply, 'but it's not for me. It's for my father.'

'Oh!' said Fred Spellacy.

Dolly Hallon thought she detected a smile. Just in case she forced one in return.

'What's his name, age and address child?'

'His name is Tom Hallon,' Dolly Hallon replied. 'His age is thirty-seven and his address is Hog Lane.'

Fred Spellacy scribbled the information onto a jotter which hung by a cord from the counter. He knew Tom Hallon well enough. Not a ne'er do-well by any means, used to work in the mill before it closed. He recalled having heard somewhere that the Hallons were honest. Honest! Some people had no choice but to be honest while others didn't have the opportunity to be dishonest.

'Can he read and write?'

'Oh yes,' Dolly assured him. 'He reads the paper every day when Mister Draper next door is done with it. He can write too! He writes to his sister in America.'

'And Irish? Has he Irish?'

'Oh yes,' came the assured response from the eleven year old. 'He reads my school books. He has nothing else to do!'

'Well Miss Hallon here's what you must get your father to do. Get him to apply for the job and enclose a reference from someone in authority such as the parish priest or one of the teachers. I don't suppose he has a *Curriculum Vitae!*'

'What's that?' Dolly Hallon asked, her aspirations unexpectedly imperilled.

'The jobs he's had, his qualifications ...'

Fred Spellacy paused as he endeavoured to find words which might simplify the vacant position's requirements.

'Just get him to put down the things he's good at

and don't delay. The position must be filled by noon tomorrow. Christmas is on top of us and the letters are mounting up.'

Dolly Hallon nodded her understanding and hurried homewards.

Fred Spellacy was weary. It was a weariness imposed, not by the demands of his job but by the demands of his wife and by the countless recommendations made to him on behalf of the applicants for the vacant position. Fred Spellacy's was a childless family but there was never a dull moment with Fred's wife Alannah always on the offensive and Fred the opposite.

Earlier that day he had unwittingly made a promise to one of the two local TDs that he would do all within his power for the fellow's nominee. Moments later the phone rang. It was the other TD. Fred had no choice but to make the same promise.

'Don't forget who put you there in the first place!' the latter had reminded him.

Worse was to follow. The reverend mother from the local convent had called, earnestly beseeching him not to forget her nominee, a genuine vessel of immaculacy who was, she assured him, the most devout Catholic in the parish. Hot on her heels came others of influence, shopkeepers, teachers and even a member of the civic guards, all pressed into service by desperate job-seekers who would resort to anything to secure the position. Even the pub next door, which had always been a *sanctum sanctorum,* was out of bounds. The proprietor, none more convivial or more generous, had poured him a double dollop of Power's Gold Label before entreating him to remember one of his regulars, a man of impeccable character, unparalleled integrity, unbelievable scholarship and, to crown all, one of the lads as well!

'Come in here!' There was no mistaking the irritation in his wife's voice. She pointed to a chair in the tiny kitchen.

'Sit down there boy!' She turned her back on him while she lit a cigarette. Contemptuously she exhaled, revelling in the dragonish jets issuing from both nostrils.

Fred sat with bent head, a submissive figure. He dared not even cross his legs. He did not dare to tell her that there were customers waiting, that the queue at the counter was lengthening. He knew that a single word could result in a blistering barrage.

'Melody O'Dea,' she opened, 'is one of my dearest friends.'

Her tone suggested that the meek man who sat facing her would grievously mutilate the woman in question given the slightest opportunity.

Again she drew upon the cigarette. A spasm of coughing followed. She looked at Fred as though he had brought it about.

'Her char's husband Mick hasn't worked for three years.'

Alannah Spellacy proceeded in a tone unused to interference, 'so you'll see to it that he gets the job!'

She rose, cigarette in mouth, and drew her coat about her.

'I'll go down now,' she announced triumphantly, 'and tell Melody the good news!'

When Tom Hallon reported for work at the sub post office at noon on the following day Alannah Spellacy was so overcome with shock that she was unable to register a single protest. When Tom Hallon donned the postman's cap, at least a size too large, she disintegrated altogether and had to be helped upstairs, still speechless, by her husband and Miss Finnerty. There she would remain throughout the Christmas, her voice fully restored and to be heard reverberating all over the house until she surprisingly changed her tune shortly after Christmas when it occurred to her that the meek were no longer meek and must needs be cossetted.

Alannah Spellacy had come to the conclusion that

36

she had pushed her husband as far as he would be pushed. Others would come to the same realisation in due course. Late in his days, but not too late, Fred Spellacy the puppet would be replaced by a resolute, more independent Fred.

Fred Spellacy had agonised all through the previous night over the appointment. In the beginning he had formed the opinion that it would be in his best interest to appoint the applicant with the most powerful patron but unknown to him the seeds of revolt had been stirring in his subconscious for years. Dolly Hallon had merely been the catalyst.

Fred had grown weary of being told what to do and what not to do. The crisis had been reached shortly after Dolly had walked out the door of the post office.

That night, as he pondered the merits of the score or so applicants, he eventually settled on a short list of four. These were the nominees of the two TDs, his wife's nominee and the rank outsider, Tom Hallon, of Hog Lane.

He had once read that the ancient Persians never made a major judgment without a second trial. They judged first when they were drunk and they judged secondly when they were sober. As he left the post office Fred Spellacy had already made up his mind. He by-passed his local and opted instead for the privacy of a secluded snug in a quiet pub which had seen better days. After his third whiskey and chaser of bottled stout he was assumed into that piquant if temporary state which only immoderate consumption of alcohol can induce.

From his inside pocket he withdrew Tom Hallon's *Curriculum Vitae* and read it for the second time. Written on a lined page neatly extracted from a school exercise book it was clearly the work of his daughter Dolly. The spelling was correct but the accomplishments were few. He had worked in the mill but nowhere else. He had lost his job through no fault of his own. Thus far it could have been the story of any unemployed man within a radius of three miles but then the similarities ended for it was revealed that Tom Hallon had successfully played the role of Santa Claus for as long as Dolly Hallon could remember. While the gifts he delivered were home-made and lacking in craftsmanship his arrival had brought happiness unbounded to the Hallon family and to the several other poverty-stricken families in Hog Lane.

'Surely,' Fred Spellacy addressed himself in the privacy of the snug, 'if this man can play the role of Santa Claus then so can I. If he can bear gifts I can bear gifts.'

He rose and buttoned his coat. He pulled up his socks and finished his stout before proceeding unsteadily but resolutely towards the abode of Dolly Hallon in Hog Lane.

He had been prepared, although not fully, for the repercussions. The unsuccessful applicants, their families, friends and handlers, all made their dissatisfaction clear in the run-up to Christmas. They had cast doubts upon his integrity and ancestry in language so malevolent and scurrilous that he was beyond blushing by the time all had their say.

One man had to be physically restrained and the wife of another had spat into his face. He might not have endured the sustained barrage at all but for one redeeming incident. It wanted but three days for Christmas. A long queue had formed at the post office counter, many of its participants hostile, the remainder impatient.

From upstairs came the woebegone cronawning of his obstructive spouse and when the cronawning ceased there came, down the stairs, shower after shower of the most bitter recriminations, sharper and more piercing than driving hail. He was very nearly at the end of his tether.

'Yes!' he asked of the beaming face which now stood at the head of the ever-lengthening queue. There was no request for stamps nor was there a parcel to be posted. Dolly Hallon just stood there, her pale face transformed by the most angelic and pleasing of smiles. She uttered not a single word but her gratitude beamed from her radiant countenance.

Fred Spellacy felt as though he had been included in the communion of saints. His cares vanished. His heart soared. Then, impassively, she winked at him. Fred Spellacy produced a handkerchief and loudly blew his nose.

THE MIRACLE OF BALLYBRADAWN

THE VILLAGE OF Ballybradawn sits comfortably and compactly atop a twenty-foot high plateau overlooking the Bradawn River. The Bradawn rises in the hills of North Cork but enters the Atlantic in North Kerry. The village with its one thousand souls lies half-way between sea and source.

In the early spring the salmon run upwards from the sea to the spawning beds, silent and silvery, shimmering and shapely. It is a most hazardous journey. Survivors are few. Man is the major enemy.

Our tale begins in the year of our Lord 1953, a climacteric span which saw the demise of Stalin, the flight of the Shah, the inauguration of Eisenhower and the conquest of Everest.

Not to be outdone, Ballybradawn was to witness its own breathtaking phenomenon shortly before Christmas of the year in question.

The spring and summer of the said year had been extremely disappointing seasons for local and visiting anglers. For some reason best known to themselves the dense schools of celebrated *salmo salar,* princes of the Atlantic, had failed to appear as had been their wont for generations, They had arrived all right but in pitifully small numbers. There was intense speculation as to what calamity might have befallen the missing fish and there was widespread belief that full compensation might be expected early during the following spring because that was the way with nature. She was known to be bountiful in the wake of insufficiency.

Indeed there were whispers from the middle of December onwards that spring fish had been sighted in the estuary. Experienced drift-net fishermen, not given to fishy tales, would bear witness to the fact that the fulsome visitors were present in considerable strength in the wide expanse where the Bradawn joined the sea.

Doubting Thomases might insist that these were spent fish on their way downwards from the spawning beds but proof to the contrary had been incontrovertible. When a spring fish plopped back into the water after a jump from its natural domain it did so with a resounding smack followed by a noisy splash which could be heard for long distances. The spent fish, on the other hand, subsided in a minor eddy on his return from a despairing leap. The resultant sound was nearly always indistinguishable from the natural noises of the river.

There were other signs to indicate the presence of spring fish. The seal population had quadrupled in the estuary and its salty precincts and, emboldened by the prospect of a fresh salmon diet, had made unprecedented incursions beyond the tidal reaches of the Bradawn where the terrified salmon sought refuge in the shallows beneath gravel banks and overhanging foliage. Here, alas, were otters who would have no misgivings about sinking sharp teeth into the living, succulent flesh of the unwary refugees from the estuary.

Further on would be poachers armed with gaffs, illegal nets, clowns' caps, cages, triple-hooked strokehauls, poisons, explosives and many other deadly devices and ruses, all aimed at terminating prematurely the brief life of *salmo salar.*

For most fish it was a one-way journey fraught with peril from beginning to end. Conservators would say that it was nothing short of a miracle that any salmon at all managed to spawn and that the species itself had survived for so long.

When word went abroad in the village of Ballybradawn that a number of spring salmon were showing in the river before their time there was great excitement among the poaching fraternity. From morn till night

41

they would discuss ways and means of supplementing their Christmas fare with the delicious flesh of an illicitly-taken salmon. Mouths watered all through their conversations as the many methods of cooking this prize product of the Bradawn River were recounted. Plans were made but none saw fruition because of the vigilance of the local water-keepers who patrolled the river day and night. All known poachers were trailed as they indulged in seemingly innocuous walks along the riverside. Towards the afternoon of Christmas Eve a man by the name of Ned Muddle chanced to be standing at one of the villages more prominent corners when he was approached by a friend who informed him about the premature arrivals. Ned expressed doubts about the veracity of his friends information.

'It's true!' that worthy assured him.

'But how come?' Ned Muddle asked.

'Some say seals,' said his informant, 'while others maintain that it's merely an error of judgment on the part of the salmon.'

A lengthy silence ensued while Ned Muddle digested the theories put forward by his friend. Ned was greatly addicted to salmon and if presented with a plate of it would not question its origins or the way it was cooked or the manner in which it was served.

Salmon, alas, were expensive and when Ned fancied fish his longings, of necessity, would generally be catered for by either herring or mackerel. Ned Muddle moved to the other side of the corner. His friend followed suit. They rested their backs against the wall while the friend held forth about the numbers and quality of the salmon which had presented themselves before their time and pointed out too how early fish fetched phenomenal prices in the country's fish markets and even a solitary kill was an assurance of drinking money for days on end.

'Yes. Yes.' Ned Muddle announced with some impatience, 'but what's all this to me?'

42

'What's it to you?' his friend expostulated incredulously.

'Why man dear,' he went on in a more mollifying tone, 'I would have thought it applied more to you than to any man.'

'Why is that?' asked an increasingly puzzled Ned Muddle.

'Don't you see?' said his friend, now facing him directly as he drove home his point, 'you are a handyman, probably the best handyman in Ballybradawn and maybe, just maybe, the greatest handyman in the country.'

Ned Muddle frowned and then smiled as he wondered if he might indeed be such a handyman, might just about be the greatest handyman in the country, the world!

'All right!' he conceded gruffly, only barely managing to conceal his pleasure, 'so I'm a handyman but what's a handyman got to do with there being salmon in the river?'

'Only a skilled handyman could make a wire cage to trap these salmon. Any ordinary handyman just couldn't do it. He would have to be the best. He would have made wire cages before this. He would have trapped salmon before this!'

'Before he went to jail you mean,' Ned Muddle suggested with a wry laugh.

The villagers of Ballybradawn would remember, but not if they were asked, when Ned Muddle went to jail and for how long and why? It had happened ten years before. He had received a three-month sentence. He had been convicted of poaching or, to be more specific, of being found in possession of explosive substances on the river bank for the express purpose of blowing the souls, if any, of the river's inhabitants to Kingdom Come and their filleted bodies to the empty larders of Ned Muddle and his wanton fellow poachers.

There had been a fine-related option but neither Ned nor his henchmen were in a position to avail of it since they were not possessed of the requisite funds. Neither were their friends, neighbours or relations so that they had nowhere to turn except to their long-suffering in-laws who would be seen as the ultimate natural redress in such contingencies except, of course, by the in-laws themselves. The in-laws, alas, for the convicted poachers, insisted that they had already pledged and paid far in excess of what might be reasonably expected of them. Ned Muddle and his accomplices served the full term.

The two friends moved away from the corner. They found themselves heading towards the cliffs which afforded a commanding view of the widest and deepest pool along the entire river. They stood with hands in pockets, their experienced eyes searching the still surface for tell-tale signs.

Minutes passed, then a quarter hour but still they stood their ground. Then it happened! A gleaming salmon, unmistakably fresh, powered itself out of the pool's centre and disappeared, almost instantly, with a mighty splash which shattered the surface of the deep pool, dispensing wavelets and ripples to both banks.

The friends withdrew their hands from their pockets and exchanged knowing glances. Words would have been superfluous and since seasoned poachers are men of few words to begin with, they hastened back to their favourite corner without the exchange of as much as a solitary syllable on the way.

'I have the makings of a cage in my back shed. 'Tis there, ready and waiting for a man of genius like yourself!'

Ned Muddle was flattered. He was not a well-loved person in the community. He was nasty to his wife and children. He was mean and he was dishonest so that words of praise rarely came his way.

In addition to being shifty, cowardly and unreliable, he had not been inside the door of the parish church, or any other church for fifteen years, since his wedding in fact, a sacrament in which he reluctantly participated and in which he might not have collaborated at all had it not been for the insistence of his in-laws-to-be who simply intimated that they would blow his brains out with a double-barrelled gun if he did not present himself at the church at the appointed time.

Despite entreaties from the parish priest and numerous curates as well as visiting missioners and pious lay people Ned Muddle steadfastly refused to conform. His neighbours would cheerfully forgive him all his other transgressions but they balked at the irreligious.

'I'll do it,' Ned Muddle announced more to himself than to his friend whose name happened to be Fred. In less than two hours they assembled the cage. Fred stood back to survey the handiwork in which he had played no more than a token part.

''Tis a work of art,' he announced, 'the village of Ballybradawn can be proud of you. Sure there's no self-respecting salmon would ignore it.'

Ned Muddle permitted himself a rare smile. Cage-making was his true metier. Even his arch-enemies the waterkeepers would concede without begrudgery that he was the best. Fred lifted the cage and bore it indoors to the bedroom which he shared with his wife. There he lovingly laid it on the large double bed which dominated the room. All that was now required was to wait until nightfall before setting out for the river where they would obstruct its flow and the passage of its denizens by constructing a low stone-built rampart from one bank to the other, leaving a gap in the middle where a strong but narrow current would attract the upgoing salmon. In this gap they would place the illegal cage which was designed to admit foolhardy fish but not to allow them egress. Large flat stones would be laid along its bottom to add weight to the structure. Otherwise, because of its lightweight composition, it would shift easily with the force of the concentrated flow.

Ned Muddle was a taciturn fellow of few words at the best of times unless, of course, he was berating his wife and family. His friend Fred, fortunately for their enterprise, eschewed conversation too except when it was absolutely necessary. Fred's wife, alas, was the opposite, a most congenial creature who, if afforded the opportunity, would spend hours at a time conversing with friends and neighbours and, when neither was available, with total strangers willing to pass the time of day. She was a woman without malice and even Fred, who rarely paid heed to her harmless narratives, would be the first to concede that his wife was incapable of misrepresentation or character assassination.

As was her wont every evening after supper, she made her way to the parish church where others like her and a small number of elderly males attended evening devotions. On the way home the good woman could not resist the waylaying of a neighbour to whom she secretly conveyed all the details of her husband's forthcoming expedition with his friend Ned Muddle.

'I know,' Fred's wife entreated her companion, 'that you won't breathe a word to a living soul.'

'Did I ever!' came the sincere response while she hurried off as quickly as her legs would take her in order to disclose the news of the planned undertaking to every Tom, Dick and Harry who would listen. Most took little notice for the good reason that previous disclosures by this particular informant had always turned out to be fabrications. Others, however, notably the wives and sweethearts of the village's established poachers, listened well and informed their menfolk. The menfolk bided their time.

No man bides his time as well as a poacher. This is because poachers, due to the secrecy imposed by their calling, are professional time-biders but how exactly do they bide it, one might well ask! The answer is by not seeming to bide it but by committing themselves wholeheartedly to a diversion far removed from poaching such as card-playing or dart-throwing or, in the case of younger, unmarried members of this close-knit fraternity, to the unremitting pursuit of unattached females.

As the evening dragged itself out Ned and Fred passed the time spying on the village resident water-keepers. There were but two. Others from outlying villages would be summoned whenever the district inspector felt it was necessary to do so. The water-keepers lived close together. The friends maintained their vigil and expressed no surprise when one keeper visited the house of the other with his wife a half-hour before midnight. Ten minutes later the four emerged together and made their way towards the parish church where the celebration of midnight Mass would begin on the stroke of midnight and where, God willing, the hearts of men and women would expand with the goodness, the charity and the forgiveness that only Christmas can generate.

As soon as they had seen the waterkeepers and their wives safely into the brightly lit bosom of the church Fred and Ned made haste to the bedroom of the latter's house where they collected the cage. Fred led the way. Ned followed with the cage. They avoided the village's main street and its attendant laneways. Occasionally as they passed isolated homes a dog would bark and as they neared the river a homebound drunkard shouted a minor obscenity as a prelude to extending the season's greetings. These they returned and continued cautiously along their way. After a mere five minutes they found themselves on the bank of the river less than two hundred yards from the village. They were somewhat apprehensive after the setting of the trap since they observed from the river bank that the light from the nearest street lamps brightened the area where they had placed it. Then, unexpectedly, from the south-west there arrived upon the scene overhead a sizable cloud which obscured the moon and brought welcome darkness to the immediate scene. It would be followed by other clouds for the remainder of their stay so that, all in all, it would be a night of inter-

47

mittent light, the kind of light beloved by poachers and others whose business runs contrary to the laws of the land.

The ideal situation, as far as Ned and Fred were concerned, would be long periods of darkness interspersed with short periods of moonlight. The pair sat on dry stones not daring to utter a word. Sometimes they would nudge each other in appreciation of the night's own distinctive sounds such as the distinct rooting of a badger or the far-off yelping of a vixen summoning a dog fox to earth. From the opposite bank came the unmistakable call of a wandering pheasant, husky yet vibrant. They listened without comment to the furtive comings and goings of the smaller inhabitants of the undergrowth and to all the other lispings, chirpings and stirrings common to the night. They listened, most of all, to the gentle background music of the running water, savouring its eddies, its softer shallows-music and leisurely, lapping wavelets. These last were almost inaudible but as distinctive, nevertheless, to the silent pair seated on dry stones, as the frailer strains of a complex symphony to the alert conductor.

Gentle breezes fanned the coarse river grasses and rustled in the underbrush whilst overhead, when the clouds gave the nod, the stars twinkled and the bright moon shone. Never had Ned Muddle entertained such a sense of sublime security. His cares had melted away under the benign influence of the accumulated night sounds. The same could be said for his friend Fred over whose face was drawn a veil of gratification, rarely enjoyed by the human species. Truly they had become part of the night. Truly were they at one with the riverside scene. There were times when they leaned forward eagerly in anticipation and times when they partially rose to their feet but it was no more than the river changing its tune as it did when the levels began to lower themselves and the lessening variations presented a different concert.

From the belfry of the parish church the midnight chimes rang pleasantly and clearly. Ned Muddle and his friend made the sign of the cross. As the final chime sounded they were both on their feet, ears strained, their faces taut.

'Did you hear a splash?' the whispered question came from Ned Muddle.

'I heard something,' his fellow poacher responded.

'Then,' said Ned Muddle a note of confidence in his tone, 'we had better take a look!'

They waded through the shallow water and there, gleaming far brighter than any of the stars over their heads, imprisoned in the cage, was a freshly arrived salmon. It turned out to be a splendid cock fish unblemished as far as they could see and shining with a radiance that belongs only to creatures of the sea. Such lustre would inevitably be dulled by a long sojourn in the upper reaches of the river but now the sea silver flashed and glittered. For a moment the creature explored its new surrounds and finding no escape began to thresh and flail for all it was worth. All, alas, was to no avail. Once a salmon enters a properly designed cage its fate is sealed.

'He's ten pounds!' Ned Muddle exclaimed with delight.

'He's twelve if he's an ounce,' his companion insisted.

Without further argument they lifted the cage and between them brought it ashore. It was Ned who extracted the struggling fish by its gills and it was Ned who located a large stone with which he smote upon the creature's poll after he had laid it on the gravelled shore and restricted its movements by holding its tail in a vice-like grip. Hands on hips, a stance copied by his companion, he stood for a while admiring the symmetry of his capture. Apart from an occasional, barely perceptible spasm, there was no movement from the fish.

'Hurry,' Ned Muddle urged his partner, 'hurry because where there's one there's more'.

'We should go while the going is good,' Fred contradicted.

'No!' Ned Muddle was adamant. Then with a chuckle he added, 'we'll hide this fellow in the bushes and go looking for his missus.'

He had but barely spoken when a whistle blew close at hand. The sound was loud and shrill and shattered not only the silence of the night but the shocked poachers as well. They stood paralysed, rooted to the ground, unable to move. The next sound to intrude upon the quiet of the night was a shot. It exploded deafeningly from a bush nearby. It was followed by a second shot. It electrified the lifeless cage-maker and his acolyte. The latter was the first to take off. Like any hunted creature he ran up the riverside. Ned Muddle who was the very personification of cowardice ran down towards the town.

'Halt in the name of the law!' The stentorian tones came from the same bush as the shots. The command only served to spur the fleeing pair to greater efforts. They ran for their lives. Finding himself unwounded after a hundred paces Ned Muddle now directed himself to where the sound of human voices in melodic union emanated sweetly from the parish church. His eyes bulging with terror he puffed his way to the only sanctuary available to him. He knew not the moment when his life might be ended with a bullet in the back. It did not occur to him at the time that the water-keepers of the Bradawn River were not licensed to bear arms nor would the local civic guards resort to such murderous tactics. It would dawn on him at a later stage that the underworld of Ballybradawn, as he was to dub the local poachers, was responsible.

As he drew nearer the church the sound of five hundred voices raised in the *Adeste*, urged him to greater effort. Breathlessly he entered the blessed refuge of light and sound. In the pulpit the parish priest, venerable and portly, conducted the singing with

50

fervour and total commitment. He suddenly lowered his hands when he beheld the stricken, dishevelled figure of Ned Muddle, poacher, wife-beater, lout and drunkard. He knew Ned well, had known him for years as a godless wretch and sacrilegious scoundrel. The parish priest's mouth opened but no sound came forth. His vast choir, without direction, was silenced as every member of the surprised congregation followed his amazed stare. They beheld Ned Muddle, his perspiring face as contrite as ever had been the face of any sinner, great or small. There were members of the gathering who could not make up their minds whether to laugh or cry. They looked to their parish priest for delivery from their indecision.

'Mirabile dictu!' the parish priest intoned the words while his eyes filled with tears. Great was the rejoicing as the congregation echoed the Latin phrase. Most were not sure of its meaning but Latin it was and as such was sacred.

After the Mass, Ned Muddle went forth into the world in peace. Need it be added that he mended his ways and came to possess the grace of God, that he became a model parent and husband and that his neighbours flocked to him when they found themselves in need of counsel or solace. He ended his days a parochial sacristan which, after the position of junior curate, is the highest ecclesiastical office in the village of Ballybradawn.

THE SCUBBLETHING

MARTIN SCUBBLE AND his wife Mary lived on the verge of the boglands. Their cottage was the last thatched habitation of its kind in that part of the world known as Tubberscubble. For generations the Scubbles had farmed the twenty acres of deep cutaway which was the total extent of their soggy holding.

Martin was the last of the Scubbles. He would say that he never missed not having children and Mary would say that she had a child.

'What is Martin?' she would ask, 'but an overgrown child that wouldn't be here nor there without me.'

Childless they might be but their's was a house that was never without children because of the constant activity in the boglands throughout most of the year. There was never a day in the summer when tea-making time came around that some boy or girl from the town or surrounding countryside did not call for hot water which was always freely available from Mary Scubble. Happy groups of turf-footers, turf-turners and stoolin-makers of all ages would seat themselves on turf sods or heather clumps under the open sky and relish every mouthful of the simple fare.

'Whatever it is about the bogland air,' the elders would say, 'it has no equal for improving the appetite.'

'I could eat frost-nails after it,' another might be heard to say.

Then in the late winter and early spring the proprietors of the bogland's many turf reeks would arrive with their horses and rails or donkeys and rails to replenish depleted stocks in the sheds and gable-reeks adjoining their homes. Always when a thunderstorm suddenly intruded or when the rain proved too drenching there was shelter and scalding tea to be had under the thatched roof of the Scubble farmhouse.

Martin and Mary Scubble were generous to a fault. All comers were welcome to their humble abode. There was, thanks be to the good God revered by both, never a cross word between them, never that is except Christmas alone when the solace beneath the thatched roof was fractured and when their conformable personalities changed utterly. Mercifully the transformation was of brief duration but it had succeeded in attracting the interest of young folk far and wide. They would arrive, unfailingly, to the boglands shortly before darkness on the Sunday before Christmas and conceal themselves in the decrepit out-houses which surrounded the farmhouse.

The annual event was known to the young generation as the Scubblething. According to their elders it had taken place for over two score years and had begun shortly after Mary Scubble had established herself as the new mistress of the Scubble holding. Some insisted that it had survived because the Scubbles had nothing else to do but the older and more perceptive of the neighbours would argue otherwise. As the neighbours grew older they paid scant attention to the goings-on at Scubbles. For them the novelty had worn off and they had come to take the whole business for granted. Not so the young folk who would nod and wink at each other eagerly as the Sunday in question approached.

'See you at the Scubblething,' they would whisper with a laugh. Many had built meaningful relationships on a first meeting at the event and there was a considerable number who had eventually married as a result. Such was its drawing power that upwards of two score of youngsters would present themselves at the Scubble environs, unknown to the principals, shortly before the winter sun reclined in, and sank into, the western horizon.

In the early years no more than a handful would hide themselves from the ageing pair, taking great care to maintain the strictest of silences before the curtain went up on the annual drama. Then as the years went by and the Scubbles grew older and feebler there was hardly any need to sustain the earlier lulls which had been so essential if they were to avoid detection by Martin and Mary.

Now in later years, the older teenagers would arrive with packs of beer and containers of Vodka. Smoking too was rife and although there was a general tipsiness to the occasion there was enough control over the proceedings to ensure that detection was avoided. Indoors Martin and Mary would settle down for the night after they had partaken of supper. Then would they seat themselves at either side of the open hearth while the rising flames from the roaring turf fire filled the kitchen with flickering tongues of light and mysterious ever-changing shadows. It could fairly be called a cosy time. Outside the young folk would silently leave their hiding places and advance to the front door and windows where they would crouch together in comforting closeness, swigging happily but noiselessly from their many bottles. Inside the ritual continued with Martin bringing his palms together and sitting erect on his sugán chair the better to fire the opening salvos.

'Do you remember last year,' said he, 'when we had that woeful argument?'

Patiently he awaited his wife's reply and when there was none he spat noisily into the fire before framing his second question.

'Do you remember,' he asked in a louder and more aggressive tone, 'the battle we had this very Sunday in this very spot at this very time?'

Still no answer from Mary. He regarded her silence as the most provocative ever imposed by a female on a long-suffering spouse and he stamped his feet noisily, one after the other, the better to register his protest.

'Dammit!' he exclaimed bitterly, 'are you deaf or what! Will you have me talking to myself for the rest of the night?'

He looked at her, his face screwed up now with

hatred. It seemed for a moment that he must seize her by the throat and put an end to her gross incitement. He rose from his chair, speechless with rage.

'I'll ask you this once,' he screeched, 'and I'll ask you no more. Do you or do you not remember our fracas last year when we argued whether it was a duck or a drake that scuttered on top of the bed when we left open the window?'

'I remember nothing of the kind,' she spat back with all the vehemence she could muster. 'I'll tell you what I remember though and it is this. It was no duck and it was no drake. What we were arguing about was whether it was a cock or a hen and ducks and drakes have nothing to do with it.'

'Damn you for a pernickety oul' woman,' Martin Scubble cried out. 'It was ducks and drakes.' He pounded the rickety kitchen table with both fists. 'I will go into any court in the land where I will swear on the Holy Book that it was ducks and drakes.'

'It costs nothing to swear,' Mary replied calmly, 'if you're a born perjurer to begin with and I'll tell you this you black-toothed oul' devil! You can swear till the book lights in your grimy paw but it won't change the fact that we were arguing about a cock and a hen.'

'Blasht you for a liar,' he shouted. 'If tables and chairs could talk and windows could give evidence you'd be transported for perjury and you'd never see hide nor light of this country again.'

Outside in the cold night air the young people hugged themselves and each other with glee. The exchanges had not lost any of their bitterness or rancour since the year before and it seemed that in spite of their great ages the Scubbles were more venomous than ever.

Inside a short silence held sway while they recharged themselves for a renewal of the conflict. They would not mention that they had the very same argument as far back as they could remember. What mattered now was to reach the climax without obstruction and to maximise their hostility towards each other. On the resumption their voices reached fever pitch. Outside the young people began to worry lest the extreme vocal exertions affect the larynxes of the contestants and bring a premature end to the performances. It happened on one occasion several years previously. The recriminations had been at their height when Mary Scubble's voice suddenly turned hoarse leaving the field of battle solely to her husband and frustrating both the Scubbles and their listeners to such a degree that all would claim later it had been the most disappointing build-up to Christmas that any of those involved could remember.

It was as though the Scubbles had suddenly realised that such a calamity was once again in the offing for, by tacit agreement, both unexpectedly paused in their detractions and defamations and drew rein as it were so that their over-worked vocal chords might recuperate. The listeners sensed that the best was about to come and they readied themselves for the final act by finishing off their near-empty bottles and lighting fresh cigarettes.

Indoors there followed barrage after barrage of the most intense, most damaging free-for-alls.

'The devil's a darling,' Mary Scubble was to say to the delight of her numerous fans on the outside. 'Oh the devil's a sweet commodity entirely when compared to some that I know, some that isn't a spit away from where I sit,'

Altogether incensed by this monstrous comparison Martin Scubble held forth with unprecedented spite.

'Repeat that before my face,' he bawled with all his might, 'repeat it that's a bitch and a backbiter's and a beggarman's baggage. Repeat it you barefaced bouncer that never wore a slip or a knickers till she was twenty-five years of age. Repeat it you virago and I promise you that I'll be vexed no more for I'll baptise you proper with a two pound pot of raspberry jam and the full chamber pot that you forgot to empty for weeks, all

56

down on the crown of your lousy head!'

Mary Scubble rose to her feet and folded her arms in a frightening pose. She threw back her grey head so that more authority might be added to her next bombardment.

'I'll do as I please,' she replied at the top of her voice, a voice that showed no sign whatsoever, of weakening, 'and while I have two feet I won't be daunted by blackguards with jam pots for my seed and breed didn't take it from the Black and Tans not to mind taking it from you and we didn't take it from the Peelers you dirty dago that would begrudge his own mother the colouring of her tea. If you don't stop your ranting straightaway, you balding battle-axe, I'll snip off your withering tassel with a stainless steel scissors.'

'Will you listen to her,' Martin Scubble extended a hand as if he was calling upon the fire in the hearth to bear witness. 'Oh what a mangy maggoty mongrel she is,' his tone soared in derision. 'Oh there is no gander as vulgar, there's no magpie as raucous and there's no badger as grey or mottled and to think she calls herself Christian!'

'Listen to what's talking,' Mary responded quickly before he had time to strengthen his advantage, 'with his rotten poll and his withered head that didn't host a black hair in forty full years and wrinkles all over him like they'd be ploughed by horses. Consecration is the only thing now that'll save you, consecration by the bishop and by the four canons of the diocese and then to steep the wretch in a barrel of holy water for nine days and nine nights till the evil inside and outside is washed away and then to have the water turned into steam and fanned away to the ends of the world for fear he'd contaminate the whole of humanity.'

Suddenly Martin Scubble cut across his wife and it seemed now that he must surely strike her but no! He resorted once more to the spoken word.

''Tis not in my breeding,' said he coldly and murderously, 'to spill female blood but yours will flow like water if you don't put a reins on that runaway tongue of yours, that black tongue that should be hauled out by the roots and ground into mince!'

Mary Scubble circled her husband like a cat contemplating a mouse.

'He's gone mental this time for sure,' she informed the tongs which she had taken into her hands. She swung the cumbersome instrument dervish-like around her head before smashing it into the fire. The bright structure collapsed about the hearth sending showers of sparks upwards and outwards. Martin withdrew towards the doorway in alarm, his hands covering his head.

'In the asylum you should be,' he thundered, finding himself safely out of reach of the deadly weapon which his unpredictable spouse now twirled around her midriff, 'but what asylum would take you with your name for mischief and agitation! 'Tis no one but myself would endure you and when I face Saint Peter he'll surely say to me: "Come in, come in Martin Scubble, my poor unfortunate man for 'tis you surely has your hell suffered down below!"'

'Houl', houl', you bothersome oul' fool,' his wife called back, 'houl', don't I catch your rotten tongue with the tongs and pull it from your festering oul' puss!'

'Shut up you harridan,' Martin shouted back but it was clear he was tiring as indeed was Mary for she had dropped the tongs and was now circling the kitchen with her head in her hands. Her next act was to place her withered hands on the table and to raise her head, ceiling-wards, before indulging herself in a fit of high-pitched, protracted pillalooing.

Martin sat himself wearily in a chair, his legs outstretched, his hands hanging limply by his sides, his mouth open. He looked the very epitome of exhaustion and dejection.

Outside, in the crisp night air, the listeners covered their laughing mouths with their hands lest their mirth filter through to the aching, exhausted couple in the kitchen.

In the surrounding countryside greyhounds and collies, terriers and beagles, filled the night with dutiful responses to Mary Scubble's lamentations. No dog barked. Rather did they cry soulfully to the moon and stars with compassion and commiseration as though they understood the plight of the demented creature from whom the sounds originated. The wailing lasted for several minutes and gradually subsided until there was silence abroad and silence indoors.

The young listeners gathered around the front door of the Scubble abode. One of the older girls knocked gently thereon but failing to elicit a response, gently lifted the latch and entered into the half-light followed by her companions. They were not surprised to see Martin Scubble seated on a chair near the fire and they were less surprised to see Mary Scubble seated on his lap. Benign smiles wreathed both their ancient faces while Martin gently stroked the grey hair of his contented spouse.

'Happy Christmas,' the young folk called out in unison.

Mary and Martin sat as though in a reverie. The young folk rearranged the fire and trooped out noiselessly. On the way home they would agree that it had been the best Scubblething ever, that there were times when it had been almost unbearable uproarious. There were some who sensed that it could be retained as an episode in their lives which would be beneficial in the long run, as a tale to be told or an experience to be savoured over and over. Others, the more sensitive, could see themselves cast in the roles of Martin and Mary in given circumstances.

All would faithfully relay the ups-and-downs of the purification ceremony which had come to be known as the Scubblething and all, no matter how insensitive or how heedless the majority might be, would conclude that maybe their own abodes could do with scubble-

things in the run-up to Christmas – their own safe, solid, seemingly happy and yet somehow lack-lustre habitations by comparison. Some would not wish such a thing for the world or so they would say. The more thoughtful believed, however, that if people burdened with the great ages of Martin and Mary needed the Scubblething on an annual basis then it would be logical to assume that everybody might need it, on some scale, especially those who insisted they didn't although not necessarily for the general delight and benefit of the young folk in the homes contiguous to Tubberscubble.

A COCK
FOR CHRISTMAS

AS WELL AS being a Christmas tale the following is also a story of romance, love and no little debauchery from the bird world. As stories go it is as true as any and it happened in my native town some time between the disappearance of the swallowtail coat and the closure of the Lartigue Railway.

It so happened that two young ladies of the so-called Ascendancy classes arrived at the Arms Hotel one September morning and asked if they might see the manager. In carefully cultivated tones from a mixture of non-Celtic origins they informed him that they required the services of the porter. On being assured that he was available they gave instructions that he was to go at once to the local railway station.

There he would collect a crate which had come all the way from Paris. The crate contained two French doves, gentler than a summer dawn and whiter than the untrodden snow.

Duly, the porter returned to the hotel where he deposited the crate upon a reading table in the foyer.

The young misses of the long-since, ousted Ascendancy were delighted and, assuming that the birds must surely be starving procured, again with the aid of the porter, the appropriate birdseed.

The doves, however, refused to dine so it was decided that they should be taken from the crate and examined. Great care was taken since it was widely accepted even then that birds had a preference for the outdoors over the indoors and would frequently take to the skies when opportunity presented itself.

Tenderly they were extracted from the crate and there was great exultation when it was discovered that they were hale and hearty and none the worse for their long journey.

The young misses had planned to take the birds to their suburban home and then, after they had familiarised themselves with the new surrounds, they would be released. It was expected that they would take speedily to their fresh environs and, in the course of time, assume the nationality of their new country. So much for the best laid schemes of doves and damsels!

In the foyer the doves were much admired but unfortunately were being passed rapidly from one pair of inexperienced hands to another so that, eventually, the inevitable happened. A garsún accidentally mishandled the cock of the pair. Did I say they were cock and hen? The cock grasped his chance and flew out of the open door.

There was consternation. A well known fainter in the company promptly collapsed so that a young lady who held the second dove in her hands lost her concentration. She had also attempted to obstruct the escape of the cock and in so doing gave the French hen the opportunity she had been waiting for. With a gentle fluttering of wings she followed her companion into the sunlight which had begun to brighten the scene outside.

In a flash the crowd in the foyer had emptied itself into the square. There was no sign of the doves. Spotters were dispatched to various parts of the town and to the nearby wood of Gurtenard which was a favourite haunt of local pigeons. Although the search went on all afternoon there was no sign of the missing pair. In their absence life was obliged to go on regardless. The afternoon drifted by and when evening arrived all hope was abandoned.

After all they were innocent strangers with no knowledge of local hawks. How then could they be expected to survive!

However, an observant corner-boy whose wont it was to gaze at the sky all day spotted them on the roof of the hotel, their gleaming whiteness contrasting sublimely with the dark grey slates.

Vainly did the hotel owner, the porter, the two Ascendancy misses and numerous other well-wishers seek to lure them down from their perches. Then one Dinny Cronin appeared on the scene for the first time. Dinny was a local pigeon-fancier and was possessed of a few magnificent specimens. Indeed in those pollution-free days the sky over the dreaming town frequently played host to large flocks of pigeons. The backyards boasted many pigeon coops and in the mornings the townspeople were frequently serenaded by soft chortlings and other manifestations of pigeonly affection.

Dinny Cronin took stock of the situation for several minutes and eventually came up with the solution.

'At home,' said he, 'I have one of the handsomest cock birds ever seen in this neck of the woods.'

On hearing that the visitors were French Dinny was taken aback but not for long.

'My bird might have no French,' said he, 'but he has the looks and he has the carriage.'

With everybody's approval he went home for the cock and returned in jig time with the pride of his flock in his coat pocket. As cocks went he was a strapping fellow, a biller and a cooer, forceful yet demure, a winner and a wooer and a charmer of pigeons from Listowel to Knockanure. Upon beholding the French arrivals he flew upwards till he was out of sight and then tumbled crazily downwards scorning all danger in the service of courtship.

After several such amorous sallies, all calculated to win the heart of the female Frenchie, he alighted on the roof. There followed some intimate bird patter, indistinguishable to all but themselves. It was apparent that there was no language barrier.

'They speak the language of love,' said Dinny Cronin, 'and that's the same in every land under the sun.' After the tender, verbal formalities Dinny Cronin's cock bird flew off and circled the nearby Catholic church three times. The Frenchies followed suit leaving the onlookers to believe that they subscribed to the same persuasion as Dinny Cronin's cock bird.

Then the trio disappeared into the fading light and were forgotten for the moment. However, when a week went by without a sign of the vanished menage there was widespread alarm.

In the ancient town business went on as usual but around the pigeon coops there was little billing and less cooing. Dinny Cronin's bird was sorely missed. Dinny himself was heartbroken for the missing cock was the pride of his flock.

Then a letter arrived from Paris for the young misses who had ordered the doves in the first place. The letter stated that the pair of doves had arrived back in the French capital accompanied by a dark stranger, a rude fellow with country manners but much admired by members of the opposite sex. There was widespread mourning for it was taken for granted that the Cronin cock would never leave the romantic capital of the known world and who could blame him!

Slowly but surely Christmas drew near with an abundance of freshly revealed humanity and goodwill. Dinny Cronin was disconsolate. It looked as if he would never see his pride and joy again. He sat towards the evening of Christmas Eve by the kitchen window pondering the joys of the past and the emptiness of the future.

Then his heart soared. He sat upright when he head the familiar chortle that had melted the hearts of a hundred doves. It was weak and it was hoarse but it was unmistakable. It was his missing cock bird. Dinny jumped to his feet and opened the kitchen window. There on the sill lay his friend, worn and exhausted after his journey from France and from countless other engagements too delicate to disclose and too numerous to mention.

He was received with joy and tears.

'My poor oul' cratur,' said Dinny Cronin, 'them Frenchies went near being the death of you.'

'Hush!' said his wife, 'mustn't youth have its fling.' Thereafter there was joy in the pigeon coops of Listowel and Dinny Cronin's prize cock wandered afar no more.

GROODLES

THE DECISION TO hold the Tubbernablaw wren-dance earlier than usual was brought about by a number of factors, the chief of which was an ominous forecast in *Old Moore's Almanac* concerning dire events in early January. First would come a blizzard so dense and driving that foolhardy travellers would not be able to see their own outstretched palms out of doors. This, according to *Old Moore*, would be followed in short order by a veritable deluge of rain and in the wake of these calamitous events there would come a frost so sharp that it would freeze the bark off the trees.

'I see nothing for it,' Billy Bonner the king of the Tubbernablaw wren-boys informed his wife on the night after Saint Stephen's Day, 'but to hold the dance tomorrow night. Otherwise we might have to wait until the spring and whoever heard of a wren-boys' dance in the springtime!'

The second factor to influence the decision was a sermon delivered by the parish priest in the nearby town on the Sunday before Christmas. He had begun as usual by admonishing wren-boys young and old and, as the sermon proceeded, whipped himself up into a frenzy while he denounced the debauchery and the drunkenness which were part and parcel of such orgies.

'If it comes to my attention,' said he, 'that a single wren-dance takes place in the New Year then woe betide the instigators. There can be no luck in a parish that allows these monstrous activities to take place. Therefore let it be known,' he concluded with upraised hands and tone hoarse with fury, 'that I shall come a-calling if word comes to my ear that the laws of church and state are being flouted.'

'If,' Billy Bonner addressed his wife who lay beside him in the bed, 'we hold no dance in the New Year we will be flouting no laws, whatever the blazes flouting is.' Beside him his wife murmured agreement. 'I therefore propose,' he declared solemnly as though he were addressing an assembly of wren-boys, 'that we go ahead with our dance tomorrow night and have done with it.'

'I second that,' his wife agreed with matching solemnity and with that she placed her arms round his neck and enquired if there was any law of church or state which might proscribe the unmentionable activities which her proximity suggested.

'Not that I know of,' Billy Bonner replied as he took her in his arms and implanted a gentle kiss on her receptive lips.

Early next morning the king of the Tubbernablaw wren-boys mounted his ancient bicycle and went westwards into his dominions in order to notify the wren-boys and wren-girls of his decision to advance the date of the wren-dance. The decree was widely applauded and in every abode to which he called he was graciously received as befitted a man of such stature. While ordinary mortals might be offered stout or beer or even whiskey out of Christmas stocks Billy Bonner was obliged to walk home leaning on his bicycle for support after the vast quantities of brandy which had been thrust upon him. Others, less valuable in the community and to the business in hand, would travel far and wide in his stead, spreading the news of the royal pronouncement. There was no dissenting voice. Billy Bonner arrived back at his home in Tubbernablaw shortly after noon. He slept for several hours before his wife deemed it prudent to rouse him from where they had cavorted so wantonly the night before. Two trusted deputies had already tackled the black mare to the common cart. All three set out earnestly for the town where they would purchase the wines, whiskies, cordials, minerals and the indispensable two half-tierces of stout which should see them safely through the festivities which would end at the breaking of day on the following morning.

Maggie Bonner had already visited the town with the wives of the two viceroys. Cooked gammons, crubins, dozens of shop loaves freshly baked, Yorkshire relish, sweet cakes and barm bracks had all been safely deposited in the vast kitchen of the Bonner farmhouse and presently the preparations for the most important element of the entire proceedings would be complete. A huge cauldron rested atop the great table. Inside sat four hocks of prime beef and a stone of freshly peeled potatoes. The three females chopped great bundles of carrots and parsnips preparatory to adding them to the cauldron's contents. A stone of onions, hard and mature and of uniform golf-ball size were peeled and quartered and then added. The Bonner soup was always the *piece de resistance* of the wren-dance and was praised far and wide for the richness and sobering effects. When all the groodles had been added the three women lifted the cauldron between them and bore it to a great fire which burned brightly beneath an iron grid specially designed and wrought by the local smith. The soup would be allowed to boil and simmer for the duration of the wren-dance until all the constituents had disintegrated and become part of the mouth-watering mixture.

'The groodles is what does it,' Billy Bonner would proclaim to his cronies as they savoured the first delicious mouthfuls of the much-lauded soup.

'Groodles,' he would go on in his homely way, 'especially parsnips, is the backbone of all soups. As faith without good works is dead so also soup without groodles is dead.'

By eight o'clock in the evening all the guests had arrived. They were carefully vetted by Billy Bonner from his vantage point in the doorway of his house and by the great grey tomcat which sat astride the warm chimney on the thatched roof of the rambling farmhouse.

There were fiddlers and melodeon players, saw and bodhrán players, didlers and concertina players, comb players and bones' tippers. There were, in fact, all kinds of traditional musicians and exponents of horn-pipe, jig and reel.

In the early part of the night unwanted gate-crashers and known trouble-makers were ejected without ceremony by the king and his faithful subjects. During these minor skirmishes which were quickly quelled several black eyes were sustained and one of the invaders' noses was broken but otherwise the wren-dance was a most harmonious occasion which was enjoyed by all who attended.

Even the intelligence officer for the local Catholic Church, also the part-time parish clerk, in his verbal report to the parish priest spent several minutes describing the character and natural consistency of the soup.

'You would want to brief the housekeeper in that respect,' the parish priest interjected jokingly. Only the clerk knew how serious he was. The parish clerk's report also included an account of the drinking and philandering although truth to tell there was little of the latter and an expected excess of the former. There had been several proposals of marriage but since these came chiefly from octo and nonagenarians as well as several drunken gentlemen who forgot that they were already married, no great notice was taken. Matters proceeded happily until midnight when the Rosary was said. Not a solitary titter was heard while the holy recital was in progress.

With regard to the serving of the food there was no formal procedure. Buffet rules were loosely applied but there was no evidence of the hogging one associates with such activities at higher levels.

Meanwhile on the outside the contents of the huge cauldron gurgled and spluttered propitiously. From time to time the king of the wren-boys and his queen,

the gracious Maggie, inspected the interior and intimated to interested parties that all was going according
to expectations.

Now all this happened at a time when motor-cars
first began to make their appearance all over the countryside so that the wives of the inexperienced drivers
entertained genuine worries about the fitness of their
partners to handle the highly deceptive vehicles when
under the influence. To counteract the effects of the
night's drinking Billy Bonner hit upon the idea of the
soup. This was the third year of the innovation. It had
proved highly successful. There had been no accidents
and no injuries and if drivers ended up in dykes and
ditches no great harm was done to the cars' occupants. In part this would have been due to the shallow-
ness of the roadside hazards but it was generally accepted that it was largely due to the reviving concoction so carefully prepared by the wives of the wren-
boys.

It was widely believed also that Billy Bonner added
a secret ingredient to the cauldron during the latter
stages of the boiling but whether this was true or not
was never really determined. There was, however, on
this particular occasion an unexpected addition to the
concoction. It was a most fortuitous supplementation
and it came about in a most unusual manner.

The top of the cauldron was covered with two flat
slabs of bogdeal. These would be removed from time to
time to facilitate stirring with a specially-rinsed, long-
handled coarse brush which Billy and Maggie Bonner
used with an expertise that made no concession to the
clotting or cloying which is so detrimental to the consistency of all such mixtures.

Now it so happened that the large grey cat which
spent most of its time stretching itself and licking its
whiskers in the vicinity of the rooftop chimney was
possessed of that curious streak which is part and
parcel of the feline make-up. As cats go, the grey Tom
was a respected figure in the countryside. In his youn-

ger days he was known to roam far and wide in search of diversion, sometimes disappearing for days at a time. Now well advanced in years he had become more of an ogler than an adventurer and contented himself by maintaining his rooftop vigil during the day and, the occasional romantic saunter apart, hugging the kitchen hearth by night. He found as many tomcats do when the years mount up that dabbling suits their age and temperament far better than the full-time fornicating in which young Toms wantonly indulge.

From early morning on the eventful day he knew that something was afoot. In his younger days he would have made non-stop forays to the kitchen, making a general nuisance of himself and as a result testing the patience of his mistress and her co-workers. Nowadays nothing short of a cat invasion would lure him from the cosy precincts of the chimney when squatted in one of his reveries. Towards evening he betook himself leisurely downwards and did the rounds of his domain. Elderly cats never indulge in the exaggerated slinking or the fancy oscillations to which younger cats are addicted. They tend to slouch and sit. They start to take things for granted and this is always a mistake.

For all his years the grey Tom leapt without difficulty on to the bogdeal slabs which covered the cauldron. The contents had not yet begun to simmer but an appetising odour issued upwards nevertheless. He peered between the bogdeal slabs but only darkness greeted his gaze. He sniffed appreciatively and would have sat for a while had not a female flung a wet dishcloth in his direction advising him at the same time that he should make himself scarce if he knew what was good for him. Unhurriedly he leaped downward and made his way to an outhouse where there was always the outside chance of an encounter with an unwary mouse. The outhouse was empty so he sat for a while preening himself in the shadows. He recalled past encounters with pretty pussies beyond the

71

bounds of Tubbernablaw and nearer home as the passing years confined him. Darkness fell while he sat immobile. With the darkness came a hard frost which decided him on his next move. He would discreetly explore the kitchen and partake of some supper before returning to lie in the lee of the chimney for an hour or two.

Indoors the festivities were at their height. The younger members of The Tubbernablaw Wren-boys' Band circulated on a regular basis with freshly filled buckets of stout drawn from the second half-tierce which had just been broached.

Pannies, mugs and cups as well as glasses, canisters, jam-pots and ewers were pressed into service. Even the grey tomcat was drawn into the revelry. He mewed for more after he had lapped up a partially-filled saucer of stout. He took his time over the second saucer, purring with uncharacteristic abandon as the drink began to take hold. Finishing the saucer he staggered out into the moonlit night. Stars twinkled in every corner of the heavens and a full moon shed its pale light on the cobbled yard where simmered the life-saving soup on its iron grid. The tomcat leaped and landed on the smaller of the bogdeal slabs. He was assailed by giddiness for a moment or two but recovered almost at once and sat himself on the larger of the slabs. He savoured the tantalising odour and held his head over the space between the slabs from where the odour emanated. Finding the larger slab a trifle too hot he removed himself to the smaller and arched himself drunkenly before composing himself catlike for a short sojourn away from the hustle and bustle of the kitchen. For the second time that day he lapsed into a reverie which saw him in his heyday seducing she-cats at every hand's turn and devouring fish and fresh liver between bouts of concupiscence. It could truthfully be claimed that there wasn't a happier tomcat in the whole of Tubbernablaw that night.

Then the hand of chance imposed itself on the

blissful scene. The sleeping Tom felt neither its fingers or its shadow. He slept, impervious to the comings and goings near the house. He did not see the pair of drunken youths who had entered the moon-drenched haggard for no other purpose than to ease the strain on their over-pressed bladders.

When the business was complete they yelled loudly in unison at the unimpressionable moon and, finding that no response was forthcoming from that quarter, looked around for some other form of diversion. It was then they beheld the sleeping cat.

'Look,' said the drunker of the pair, 'at the neck of that cat, sleeping on top of the soup.'

'Let him be,' said the other, 'what harm is he doing?'

'Suppose,' said his companion in an outraged tone, 'that he piddles into the soup or maybe even worse!'

The pair tiptoed noiselessly until they reached the turf rick which dominated the far end of the haggard. Here they located two small black turf sods and, taking aim, dispatched both in the direction of the slumbering Tom. The chance of either reaching the target, in any reckoning, must surely attract odds of thirty-three to one. The first of the small but rock-hard missiles veered left and landed harmlessly on the farmyard dung-heap. The second sped unerringly towards the victim as it raised its head, instinctively alerted by a sixth sense. It was, alas, too late. The sod landed on the crown of its head and laid it senseless. It slumped and then slid between the bogdeal slabs. It subsided without a miaow into the simmering soup.

The buck who pelted the fatal sod turned at once and rejoined the revels in the kitchen. He salved his conscience by making the sign of the cross and spitting over his left shoulder. Wisely, he and his friend decided to keep the story of the tomcat's demise to themselves. Why waste a perfectly good barrel of soup, give or take a cat!

Such were the philosophies that were in the air at

that time and in that place. A cat could be replaced in due course but a cauldron of soup, in the circumstances, could not. In the kitchen the revelry went on unabated until dawn. Then at eight forty-five in the morning Billy Bonner stood on a chair and announced that it was time to bring the proceedings to a close. The announcement was made seven hours and fourteen minutes after the demise of the family cat. At first there were some minor protestations but common sense soon prevailed especially when the head of the house reminded his listeners that the soup was ready and would be served forthwith, that it would be served under the wide and starry sky and that those who were interested should proceed without delay into the night bringing with them whatever vessels were at hand. There was an immediate exit. Mugs, cups and canisters were waved aloft as the delighted revellers cheered with all their might in anticipation of the incomparable composition which awaited them.

There were gasps and cheers and screams and diverse exclamations of delight as cup after mug after canister of soup was consumed. The steam from hundreds of mouths, nostril and receptacles ascended the frosty air while from the cauldron itself there issued a perpendicular column which disappeared into the heavens overhead and tempted the moon herself to indulge in an unprecedented descent from her starry climes.

Standing to one side in the shadows were the youths who had so unceremoniously dispatched the cat to the hereafter. They hugged their sides with glee as they eagerly awaited the convulsions and upheavals which they felt must inevitably assail the soup drinkers of Tubbernablaw and its hinterland. They waited but all that transpired, as the time passed and the morning brightened, was a clamorous demand from all present for more soup. As things turned out there was plenty for everybody.

When the cauldron was drained of its last drop

Billy Bonner and a retainer spilled out the bare bones that remained on to the frozen ground. The cat-killers edged forward but before they could draw a solitary person's attention to the fact that they had all partaken of cat soup and that the evidence was there to prove it the three household dogs, a red setter, a suspect Collie and a retired coursing greyhound had fled the scene with mouthfuls of bones ranging from the head of the grey tomcat to the denuded hock bones of bullock and heifer. They would return almost at once to recover the few lesser bones that remained and add them to the others secreted where none but themselves would find them.

Search as they might, the disgruntled cat-killers failed to find a trace of their victim.

Nothing remained, not an eye nor a tooth nor a single, solitary cat's whisker nor any evidence whatsoever of any one of the nine lives which are the God-given right of all cats great and small.

THE GREAT CHRISTMAS RAID AT BALLYBOOLEY

IT ALL HAPPENED back in 1920 when those heinous wretches known as the Black and Tans were hell-bent on maiming, murdering and all forms of diabolical destruction and showing themselves to be true credits to the calabooses from which they had been released in order to serve their country and shoot innocent Irish people.

No day passed without some skirmish or other between the dreaded invaders and the brave boys of the North Kerry Flying Column. The more notable of these encounters are suitably remembered in song and story but none more so than the great Christmas raid at Ballybooley. True, this singular event has its controversial side but in this respect it must be said that no two accounts of any battle are similar in every detail.

The year in question produced one of the driest summers ever recorded. The hills, in fact, turned brown. On the turf banks the sods dried of their own accord which was a blessing indeed to youthful turf-turners and stoolin-makers who were free to spend the long summer days by river and stream or lazing in carefree groups in woodland and meadow.

Nobody, however, can put forward the claim that Mother Nature spreads her output indiscriminately and as though to prove this point beyond doubt she presented the North Kerry countryside with a succeeding Christmas of unprecedented bitterness and savagery.

Hail, rain and snow were commonplace whilst, in

between, Jack Frost worked overtime. The tinder dry turf of the summer made no battle in the gusty hearths of cottage and farmhouse and people were wont to say, not for the first time, that if there was anything worse than turf that was too wet then surely it was turf which was too dry. Many of the roadside reeks were consumed before Christmas. Rusty saws and axes were resurrected for the felling of timber. Fuel theft grew rife as the winter wore on.

In all the bogland area perhaps the most practised lifter of the unguarded sod was a man by the name of Micky Dooley. He was well-known to all and sundry as a professional turf thief. All through November and December when the moon shone fitfully, if at all, he would betake himself with ass and rail to a convenient bog there to ply his shifty trade.

Under cover of darkness he would fill his rail from ill-made reeks whose appearances would not be affected by the disappearance of an ass-rail of turf. It was different with well-made reeks. A solitary sod out of place and the owner was immediately alerted.

A well-made reek was a match for anything be it thunder, gale or turf thief. Each sod was so close to the next and each corner so smoothed and well-constructed that even the absence of a single cadhrawn would be easily detected. Consequently turf thieves shied away from well-made structures and concentrated on the badly-made, misshapen ones. It was to these latter on the dark and stormy nights around Christmas that Micky Dooley directed his ass and cart. His target, of course, would have been thoroughly reconnoitred beforehand. One might see him sauntering casually in the distance, his head averted from roadside reeks, his gaze fixed steadfastly in front of him as though reek-rape was the farthest thought from his mind. Yet without once inclining his head or slowing his gait he absorbed every detail of his night-time objective.

His attention might seem to be fixed on a flock of

wheeling plover in the skies overhead or rapt in admiration at a particular rampart of cloud but all the while he stored detail after vital detail for future reference.

He would have to discover in the little time available to him if there was room for donkey and cart at the bogland side of the reek or if the reek had already been gutted by storm and above all to determine the quality of the turf. It was essential that it resemble in texture, size and shape the inadequate supply he had harvested for his own use in case a suspicious reek owner decided to investigate.

When his rail was filled he would skilfully rearrange the area which he had plundered so that it was always next to impossible to detect the loss. This was an art in itself. His efforts were always constricted by the absence of light. As a result he worked like a man demented whenever a ray of moonlight filtered through the flying clouds. Moonlight is the natural enemy of the night-raider but he needs a little now and then to be going on with.

Largely, however, Micky worked by the feel, waiting for a token of moonlight to add the finishing touches. He never took more than one rail from any reek and this was the real secret of his success. Suspect he might be but there was no proof and so long as he confined his looting to reasonable quantities his thieving excursions were taken for granted.

Those whose reeks escaped molestation were fond of saying it was a poor bog indeed that couldn't support a solitary turf thief.

Then came a fearful night shortly before Christmas. The north-eastern gales bore down the sky furiously whipping and flailing the already-tormented countryside. Sitting by his fire Micky Dooley decided that it was an excellent night for an enterprising fellow like himself. Reluctant though he was to forsake his warm hearth the night was heaven-sent for his purpose.

Nobody in his right mind, a turf-thief apart, would

venture abroad under such conditions and who was to say but the weather might take a dramatic turn for the better and so curtail his outdoor activities when they might most be needed. He resolved to venture forth.

He tackled the unwilling donkey to the ancient cart, assembled the rail thereon and, to ensure silence, liberally plastered the axle screw-nuts with car grease. He bound himself thoroughly against the elements and set forth on his journey.

A worse night he had never experienced. Within minutes his gloved hands were freezing, the fingers stripped of circulation. He closed his eyes against the storm and blindly followed the donkey. He would have turned back after the first quarter mile but he reminded himself sensibly that after a storm comes a calm and since his turf stocks were almost exhausted he simply had to make the most of his opportunity.

Slowly, patiently, man and beast battled against the savage blasts until both were on the threshold of exhaustion. At length they arrived at the bog lane where the several remaining reeks stood awaiting the inevitable. As they reached the first of these, one which he had rifled a bare fortnight before, the donkey stopped dead and despite all Micky Dooley's urgings refused to proceed against the gale-force wind. Micky knew that the poor animal had reached the end of its tether. There was nothing for it but to turn round and proceed homewards. At least they would have the wind behind them. He backed the donkey into the lee of the reek. There it would regain its wind for the return journey. As he waited, in the bitter cold, the combination of temptation and habit proved too much for Micky Dooley.

'All I'll take is a few sods,' he told himself, 'for since I have raided this reek before, to take any more would be folly.'

Alas his rapacious instincts prevailed and in no time at all he had the rail filled and clamped.

The days passed with no abatement in the weather. Soon the rightful owner of the turf put in an appearance with a horse and cart and proceeded to fill his rail. The first thing he noticed, upon his arrival, was a sizable declivity at the reek's rear. A grim smile appeared on his weather-beaten face. This merely proved to be the prelude to the heartiest of laughs and, this in turn, was followed by a gleeful shout and a rubbing together of the palms of the hands.

For several moments he cavorted delightedly around the roadway. For long he had suspected Micky Dooley. He estimated that over the years the turf thief had relieved him of twenty ass-rails at the very least. When, a few weeks before, he visited the reek his suspicions had been aroused upon beholding a small mound of fresh donkey dung close by the reek. A sure sign, this, that a donkey had dallied there.

Carefully he had inspected the reek but could find no sign of interference. This did not surprise him in the least as it was not Micky Dooley's wont to leave evidence of his visits.

The proprietor of the reek was forced to concede that Micky was without peer in the art of restructuring turf reeks. He would have dearly loved to lay hands on him there and then if for no other purpose than to strangle him.

As he filled his rail he considered ways and means of snaring the thief. Suddenly an inspired albeit murderous notion struck him. Frequently he played host to men on the run and sometimes they concealed their guns and ammunition on his property. That night he revisited his reek, his pockets filled with live ammunition. With the utmost care he inserted a score of bullets in the softer of those sods which occupied the weakest corner of the reek. Now a fortnight later he congratulated himself on his foresight. He had gambled that the thief would pay a second visit because of the severity of the weather and he had won. That night in bed he conveyed the tidings to his wife.

'I have prepared,' he said, 'a terrific Christmas gift

80

for Micky Dooley. It's a gift he'll never forget till the day he dies and I have to say that no man deserves it more.'

He then told her about the live ammunition embedded in the sods.

'Oh sweet Mary Immaculate,' his wife cried out clutching her rosary beads, 'suppose someone is struck by a bullet.'

'I don't care,' said her husband, 'if the hoor is blown to Kingdom Come. He'll never steal another sod from me one way or the other.'

Chuckling to himself he turned over on his side and slept the sleep of the just. His wife prayed into the small hours faithfully accompanied by the sonorous snores of her husband. She beseeched every saint with every prayer in her repertoire that no harm would befall the household of Micky Dooley.

Less than a week later, on Christmas Eve to be exact, Micky was seated in front of a roaring fire with his wife and children and a neighbour who had called to exchange titbits of gossip in return for basking cold shins before the glowing sods. Outside the wind howled and hissed whilst hordes of unruly hailstones hopped and danced on road and roof.

'God bless us,' said the female neighbour, by name Maggie Mulloy, 'isn't a good fire the finest thing of all.'

'True for you Maggie,' her host responded. 'I wouldn't swap a good fire for a bottle of whiskey.'

There they sat, happily contemplating the leaping flames, savouring the warmth and comfort of the hearthside. A happier scene could not be imagined. A black buck cat, fat and sleek, sat at his master's feet while the children intoned their rhymes in a drowsy hum that added to the somnolent atmosphere of the fireside scene.

'Thanks be to God for a turf fire,' Maggie Mulloy said under her breath and then in a louder tone, 'and thanks to them that has the heart and the nature to share that same.'

81

Micky Dooley accepted the compliment as befitted such a magnanimous benefactor.

'Tut-tut,' he said dismissively, 'tut-tut.'

The cat purred, the women nodded and Micky Dooley reached forward a foot to restore a wayward sod which had fallen too far from the fire. The sparks shot upwards in a bright display which boasted every conceivable shade of red. Then suddenly all hell broke loose. The first bullet smashed into the paraffin lamp which hung by a chain from a central rafter between two flitches of yellowing bacon. There followed immediately a minor explosion after which the light went out.

The second bullet smashed into the dresser and shook it to its foundations as well as sending saucers, cups and ware of all sorts flying about the kitchen. The third bullet went straight between the two eyes of the cat. Without as much as a mew he stiffened and expired where he lay, a taunting parody of the nine lives supposed to be his right.

For several seconds after the first shot Micky Dooley remained rooted to his chair, unable to move. His mouth opened and closed but no sound emanated therefrom. He was shocked to his very core. A bullet whistling past his ear brought a sudden end to his inactivity. Ignoring the cries of the women and children he bolted for the bedroom where he barricaded the door behind him and dived straightaway under the bed.

He shut out the appalling din in the kitchen by the simple expedient of thrusting a finger into either ear. His heart raced so violently that he feared for its continued beating. No heart, he felt, could continue at such a pace without coming to a sudden and untimely halt. Trembling, he invoked the aid of his dead mother after which he loudly beseeched the Sacred Heart to succour him in his final agony.

In the kitchen there was absolute bedlam. The screams were deafening. Neighbours, near and far,

82

were brought to their doors by the mixture of shots and cries of human torment.

"Tis the Black and Tans,' one terrified listener called out. 'There's a battle on in Ballybooley.'

His cry was quickly taken up and in jig time every door and window in the district was barricaded. Lights were doused and Rosaries recited. Holy water was sprinkled here, there and everywhere.

Meanwhile back at the Dooley kitchen three more bullets went off. The first of these passed through the window. The other two ricocheted up the chimney and spent themselves harmlessly on the night air. Mercifully none of the kitchen's occupants was injured. A sustained silence ensued but a longer period was to pass before Micky Dooley opened the bedroom door. At that precise moment the last bullet exploded from the fire and pierced the upper of his left boot. It lodged in his instep. He fell to the floor, a cry of anguish on his lips.

'They got me,' he screamed.

His wife and children knelt by his side while Maggie Mulloy breathed an Act of Contrition into his ear. After a while, when it was clear that the shooting had ended, they lifted him on to a chair where he sat with the injured leg resting on another chair. Maggie Mulloy, who lived less than a stone's throw away, had gone and returned in a thrice with a noggin of whiskey. Micky disposed of it without assistance. The eldest of the children was dispatched to a neighbour's house with the curt instructions that a doctor and priest were to be contacted at once.

Outside the wind had abated and soon neighbours from every house within a two mile radius converged upon the house. The same question formed on the lips of every last one of them. What had happened?

'We were ambushed,' Micky Dooley explained.

'But why?' the communal question came.

The wounded man shook his head knowingly and brought a silencing finger to his lips indicating that there was more involved here than met the eye.

'We were ambushed,' he exclaimed to every newcomer.

'By whom?' the question came automatically on the heels of the others.

'Tans,' was Micky Dooley's immediate response. He kept repeating the word embellishing it every so often with choice adjectives. Eventually and inevitably the man who had planted the bullets arrived upon the scene. Tentatively he thrust his head inside the door.

'Black and Tans,' Micky disembarrassed him before he had a chance to apologise and spoil the entire proceedings. The bullet-planter nodded vigorously relieved beyond measure that no one had been killed. As it was, if the truth were to become known, the least for which he would be held accountable would be attempted murder.

'Tans it was,' he confirmed. 'Didn't I see them with my own two eyes and they making off down the road.'

Micky Dooley bent his head in gratitude and relief. It was only then that he noticed the dead cat. He lifted the stiffening form to his lips and kissed it on top of the head which was a change indeed for the only other part of the creature's anatomy with which he had any previous contact was its posterior whenever he applied one of his hobnailed boots to that sensitive area for no reason whatsoever.

'My poor cat,' he called out while his eyes calefacted huge tears to suit the occasion. One by one the neighbours departed, arguing heatedly as to why such a savage attack had been made on a household which had no apparent connection with the Freedom Fighters.

They came to the only conclusions possible. The Tans had been seen by a reliable witness. They were, therefore, responsible for the attack. They would not have carried out the attack unless Micky Dooley was a dispatch carrier or was in the habit of secretly harbouring the men on the run.

Apart from Micky only one man knew the truth and that man's lips were sealed. It was that or subject himself to the possibility of a stiff prison sentence. There was no point in taking such a gamble. One thing was certain. Micky Dooley would never interfere with one of his reeks again. Others yes but not his. That had been the primary point of the exercise.

Time passed and word of the raid spread. The account was handsomely embroidered with the passage of the years so that, in the end, it transpired that Micky Dooley had single-handed, armed only with a double-barrelled shotgun, routed a score of Black and Tans killing none but wounding several while he himself would be a martyr to a pronounced limp for the remainder of his life. His neighbour Maggie Mulloy came to be revered throughout the countryside. Had she not fought by her neighbour's side? None begrudged her the paltry state pension and service medals which a grateful government had conferred on all those who had participated in the Fight for Freedom.

Micky Dooley fared better. Because of his limp he was awarded, in addition to his service pension, a handsome disability allowance which left him secure for the remainder of his days.

Maggie Mulloy eventually came to believe her own story. Without doubt, on a gusty winter's night under a fitful moon, shadows may be easily transformed into human shapes. No great effort is afterwards required to deck them in uniforms. Far from abandoning his old ways Micky Dooley redoubled his raids upon vulnerable turf ricks. Now he stole with impunity. Wasn't it his right he told himself. Didn't he single-handed defeat a company of Black and Tans! By God if he wasn't entitled to a few sods of somebody else's turf who was! Wasn't he one of the two surviving heroes of the Battle of Ballybooley. The bullet-planter would never mention the Christmas gift again, not even to this wife.

From time to time strangers visited Mickey Dooley's house to inspect the holes left by the bullets and to view the almost fatal wound upon his instep. Veneration was also paid to the memory of the cat whose life was ended so tragically in the service of its master. As Micky Dooley used to say when reminded of the creature's demise: 'Greater love no cat hath than the cat who lays down his life for his friends.'

THE MAGIC STOOLIN

I WAS TEMPTED for a while to call this story *A Christmas Barrel*. Everybody, I told myself, has heard of *A Christmas Carol* so why not *A Christmas Barrel*. My wife thought the title too stereotyped when I submitted it for her approval. It was then I thought of *The Magic Stoolin* and, if you care to continue, you will see why.

Times were never worse in the bogland of Booleenablawha. On the run-up to Christmas the county council had reluctantly suspended all roadwork and there was no likelihood that it would resume before spring.

Of all the seven families surviving on the bog road, Jack Tobin's was the hardest hit. The others had grown-up sons and daughters working in England and America but the eldest of Jack's cúram was only ten and the youngest still in swaddling clothes.

There was some consolation to be drawn from the fact that there would be plenty to eat over the twelve days of Christmas. Jack had seen to that. He had disposed of ten stoolins of dry turf in the nearby town. Each stoolin was the equivalent of a clamped horse rail and each had fetched a pound in the market place. Twelve stoolins remained in the bog, impervious, because of their perfectly tapering design and solid structure, to the rain, sleet and hail which would bombard them until the advent of May.

Jack might have disposed of three or four more and thus provided himself with the wherewithal for Christmas drink but this would mean sparser fires providing the winter wind with the openings it needed to freeze the toes and chill the blood. With Jack and his wife Monnie the children always came first.

'If we pinch and pare,' Monnie had whispered as

they lay on the feather bed two weeks before Christmas, 'we might rise to a dozen of stout and a half-bottle of whiskey and maybe a few minerals for the children. There's three bottles of cheap sherry left after the wake and that will do the women.'

Jack's father had expired the previous summer from nothing worse than simple senility and the subsequent wake had made massive inroads into their insubstantial savings. The couple's concern with the drink stocks did not stem in any way from their own desires for intoxicating liquor although Jack could never be charged with missing a Sunday night at the crossroads pub. Monnie would truthfully declare that drink never troubled her. The problem arose because of an age-old custom whereby each of the seven houses in Booleenablawha hosted in turn, over the Yuletide period, a modest reception for the other six.

It wasn't that the hostesses vied with each other or that drinking was excessive but it had never been known, even in the blackest of black times, that a household had run out of drink. No other hostings, apart from wakes, weddings and wren-dances, could possibly be countenanced in the hard-pressed community at any other time of year.

If the neighbours but knew of Jack's position they would have cheerfully brought a sufficiency of drink with them but this was the last thing Jack and Monnie wanted. Jack also knew that he might borrow a pound or two from a friend or that he might secure credit at the crossroads where he was known but this wasn't his way either.

The pucker would remain unsolved until the week before Christmas. The morning rain had cleared and a fresh breeze rustled in the roadside alders. Jack Tobin went among his stoolins carefully selecting the drier, darker sods for his Christmas fires. A past master in the high art of stoolin rearrangment Jack's turf castles, as his children called them, would not disintegrate under the buffeting winds and driving rains.

As he slowly filled his ass-cart he was surprised to see the heavily-laden lorry making its way over the narrow, bumpy bog-way. Jack waved at the driver and the driver waved back. Then the lorry passed by, its precious cargo of wooden porter casks swaying dangerously because of the uneven contours of the quaking road.

The man who had waved at him, Jack felt, would be a relief driver hired temporarily for the busy Christmas period who would be unfamiliar with the terrain. Otherwise he would not have departed from the main road and chosen a shorter but far more hazardous itinerary. Then it happened! There was, a hundred yards further down the road, a hump-backed bridge, covered with ivy and ancient as the road itself. A cannier driver would have slowed down. As the lorry passed over, its body was suspended for a brief while when the cab dipped on the downward side. As the airborne back wheels struck the roadway a barrel leaped upward and outward and fell onto the soft margin, rolling backwards until its progress was arrested by a sally clump. Jack Tobin immediately abandoned his labours and ran towards the roadway, furiously waving and calling out at the top of his voice in a vain effort to attract the driver's attention. Then the lorry was gone. Jack Tobin found himself confronted with an untapped half-tierce of approved porter.

A half-tierce, as every wren-boy knows, contains one hundred and twenty-eight pints of dun-dark, drinkable, delight-inducing porter, porter so profuse that the drinking folk of Booleenablawha would be hard put to consume it in the round of a single night. Jack Tobin stood without moving for several minutes. There was much to be resolved. Meanwhile he would roll the barrel deeper into the sally clump lest it attract the attention of passing vagabonds and heaven knows what fate.

That night as they sat by the dying fire, with the children sound asleep in their beds, Jack informed his wife for the first time of the day's happenings and the location of the sally-girt windfall.

Monnie Tobin lifted the tongs and discovered a number of small bright coals hidden in the ashes.

After she had rearranged the fire she pointed the tongs at her spouse in order to lend emphasis to her asessment of the situation.

'First thing in the morning of Christmas Eve,' she said, 'you will cycle to town and take yourself into McFee's the wholesalers. Find out if they're missing a half-tierce of porter. If they are the barrel will be returned. If not we'll see.'

They spoke long into the night concerning the state of the family finances but despite all her economic wizardry, all her penny-pinching and self-sacrifice, there was no obvious way the situation could be improved.

Despite the most assiduous of searches the clerical staff at McFee's could find no record of a missing barrel. No complaint had been filed by a shortchanged customer and the stock in their storehouse tallied accurately with the advice notes.

'Why?' asked the firm's chargehand with a laugh 'is it how you found a barrel?'

'No,' came the instant reply. 'It's just that there was a rumour going the rounds.'

Later, as night was falling on the boglands of Booleenablawha, Jack and Monnie Tobin announced to the children that they were taking a stroll. When they returned there would be a distribution of lemonade and biscuits to celebrate Christmas.

Out of doors a crisp breeze blew steadily from the south-west. Overhead a full moon shed its pale light on the rustling boglands. Now and then passing clouds obscured its rays. It proved to be an ideal night for what Jack and Monnie had in mind.

At the sally clump where lay hidden the prized half-tierce they paused and awaited one of the night's darker spells. Even then they maintained a vigil for several moments. Then when the darkness was at its most impenetrable Jack rolled the barrel from its place of concealment and, aided by his partner, pushed it slowly to where a narrow passage led on to the turf-bank where stood the twelve unassailable stoolins.

Inside the wooden cask the porter chuckled and gurgled tantalisingly. After a few moments the interior noises stopped. Jack Tobin rightly surmised that the rolling movements had brought a head to the barrel's contents. His mouth watered at the prospect of savouring the first mouthful of the cherished brew.

He had not come unprepared. In his pocket was a brass tap, a relict from numerous wakes. Earlier he had deposited a hastily-hewed wooden mallet at the blind side of a specially chosen stoolin. The mallet would serve nicely to drive the tap home when the barrel was in place. Jack had the additional foresight to bring along a brace and bit together with a tapering wooden spike which would be used to plug the bung-hole made by the former in order to facilitate an expeditious flow from the tap.

Jack's special skills and foresight with regard to regulating the condition and the drawing of porter came from long experience. In addition to the annual wren-dances which flourished throughout the region there were countless wakes where several porter barrels might be on flow at the same time. Consequently there were few houses in the countryside without some sort of porter tap and a brace and bit.

As in all trades there were the highly-skilled and the botchers. With so much hinging on a successful outcome it would have been unthinkable to entrust the tapping of a full barrel containing such an irreplaceable commodity to an incompetent! Only the practised and the proven were elected to take charge of such a momentous undertaking. Jack Tobin was one of these.

On their arrival at the stoolin he quickly removed two-thirds of the upper body. Then with a mighty effort he lifted the half-tierce and laid it horizontally on the carefully structured base. Without hurry he bedded it firmly, but lovingly, so that it would lie still during the tapping. One, two, three rapid, accurate, beautifully-timed strokes and the tap was firmly embedded in the barrel.

Without undue haste Jack Tobin remade the stool-in all around the recumbent cask. The demands of this difficult task brought out the artist in him. True, he was aided by a full moon but it is the touch as much as the perception that makes the difference between a great stoolin-maker and an indifferent one.

Smearing a liberal handful of turf mould over the exposed tap he extracted a tin pannikin from his coat pocket. Now would come the acid test. Those in the countryside who were partial to porter and they were many would quite rightly aver that every content of every barrel tasted differently. Some were too highly conditioned and some were too flat. Some carried a bitter tang whilst, worst of all, others were casky and decidedly unpalatable. Casky barrels were rare and were always replaced by the brewing house. Unfortunately, because of the nature of its acquisition, no such redress would be available to Jack Tobin if the lost barrel was tainted.

He looked upward first at his heavenly ally, still free of cloud and undisputed queen of the heavens. What if the barrel was filled with water or with cleansing fluid! Holding the pannikin under the spout he turned on the tap. A powerful jet of sweetly-smelling porter foam knocked the pannikin from his hand. Quickly he turned off the tap and reclaimed the pannikin.

At his second attempt he only partially turned on the tap. The diminished outflow, still powerful, smote merrily against the bottom of the pannikin so that Jack was obliged to slant the shallow vessel in order to avoid a spillage. When the pannikin was filled he allowed it to rest atop the stoolin so that the froth might subside and the porter proper accumulate beneath.

When he judged the time to be ripe he handed the
pannikin to his wife. First she tasted and then, delighted by the first impressions, swallowed heartily, de-
claring when the pannikin was drained, that she had
never tasted the likes in all her days.

'It's like cream,' she announced, wiping her lips,
'only nicer.'

After several pannikins each they recovered their
possessions and, hand in hand, returned homewards,
their happy way benignly lighted by the liberal moon.

'Did you ever taste the likes of it?' Monnie Tobin
asked as they neared home.

'Never!' Jack assented as he squeezed her hand
and placed a frothy kiss on her upturned lips, frothy
too. That night, full of porter-induced, seasonal man-
suetude, Jack and Monnie Tobin sang the gentle songs
of their youth for their delighted children.

Time passed until all that remained of the twelve
days of Christmas were two. It was the night the
Tobins played host to their neighbours all. Never was
there such a night. Every half-hour or so Jack Tobin
would disappear, through his back door, bearing two
small milking buckets. In a matter of minutes he
would be back again with two buckets brimful of the
most nourishing, the most savoury, the most flavour-
some porter ever consumed in that part of the world or
so the neighbours said.

Naturally they questioned its origin when it loosen-
ed their tongues. Jack informed them that it had come
from the city of Limerick through the good offices of a
calf jobber who was partially indebted to him for having extended credit to him earlier in the year.

And how had he transported it was the next
question tabled? Oh by milk churn of course and had
not Jack carefully transferred it from the jobber's
churn to his own where it had, slowly but surely, ac-
quired the immaculate condition which set it apart
from the less exhilarating porter of former years! More
evidence, however, was required by the discerning

elders of Booleenablawha and, indeed, more evidence was forthcoming.

'And pray!' asked Jack's immediate neighbour, a man with an insatiable appetite for information, regardless of its veracity, 'could you tell us the name of the tavern where this porter was purchased?'

The question caught Jack unawares. There was also the lamentable fact that he did not know the name of a solitary tavern in the city of Limerick for the good reason that he had never been there.

'The name of the tavern you say!' He pretended to ponder.

It was his wife who came to his aid.

'The name of the tavern,' said Monnie Tobin, without batting an eyelid, 'is the Magic Stoolin.'

'The Magic Stoolin!' the neighbour repeated, 'sure don't I know well where it is.'

The last thing the poor fellow wanted to profess was ignorance of this well-known watering place which was surely known to man, woman and child in the city of Limerick and other places besides.

As it turned out the Magic Stoolin was known to several other accomplished liars in the gathering who had never been to Limerick either and also to their womenfolk who were in the habit of supporting them, without question, in all manner of spurious claims and submissions over the years.

From such unfailing corroborations are lasting marriages nurtured, are peace and probity maintained within the family and are Christmases revered and relished in the simple homesteads of Booleenablawha.

THE ORDER OF
MacMOOLAMAWN

THE WREN, THE wren, the king of all birds
On Saint Stephen's Day he was caught in the furze
Although he was little his family was great
Rise up landlady and give us a treat.

For those who found Christmas Day a trifle stifling Saint Stephen's Day or Boxing Day came as a boon to the residents of the town. There were some who simply called it Wren-boys' Day for the very good reason that from morning onwards until the public houses closed that night the wren-boys of the rustic hinterland converged on the streets and square. They came singly, in pairs, in small groups and great bands, bringing with them their songs and dances immemorial to gladden the heart and disperse the post-Christmas queasiness. They came in traditional costume of calico with tinsel-bedecked, peaked caps and a wide range of musical instruments, most notable of which was the goat-skin bodhrán.

They played, sang and danced their merry way by highway and byway until their cashiers and captains decided that sufficient monies had been gathered to cover the cost of the annual wren-dance which would be held in early January.

Those wren-boys and, indeed, wren-girls who chose to travel singly and in pairs retained the spoils for their own uses and benefits. Some used them to discharge outstanding debts while more availed of the windfalls to buy boots or shoes for themselves and their offspring. The remainder which represented the majority drank their fill without let-up until the proceeds had vanished. None, not even the virtuous, pointed the finger of denunciation at the profligates who might have spent their earnings more profitably for, in that place and in that time, life was often tedious and diversions few.

Our tale concerns two elderly wren-boys who were martyrs to the annual squandermania aforementioned. The years, as is the wont of years, had taken their toll on the pair and although the vigour had departed their steps they resolutely refused to submit themselves to infirmity. Both have now passed on to that happy clime where the gentle drumming of goat-skin bodhráns forever assails the ear and wren-dances are celebrated on a non-stop basis. This would be their concept of heaven and why not! Hath not the Lord said 'In my father's house there are many mansions'. Then it must be remembered that life itself isn't exactly a wren-dance so that men may dream of the everlasting one.

Anyway, there they were, our intrepid friends away, away back in 1939 as drunk as two brewery rats on the very evening of Christmas Day. All around them the other illicit public house patrons spoke in rich whispers about the vagaries of life and the ultimate futility of excessive thrift, about wren-dances past and wren-dances to come and, in between, about brotherly love. They toasted friendship and loyalty and they clinked their glasses gently, vowing that they would surely meet again in the same venue at the same time on every succeeding year until they were called to another place. All they craved was that it be half as good as the present one.

Outside on the streets the forces of law and order paused in their perambulations outside the frontages of suspect public houses and listened intently or pretended to listen intently and then, satisfying themselves that no intoxicating drink was being served within, proceeded on their majestic way without the batting of an eyelid or the breaking of a step.

In those days there was in every town and village a public house or even two which would always remain open on Christmas Day. The publicans in question, otherwise above reproach, would proffer the excuse that they could not bear to see so many downcast souls suffering from untreated hangovers wandering the streets and laneways without hope of recovery. Out of the goodness of their hearts and nothing more these soft-centred public house proprietors would discreetly admit the needy and the suffering provided they were versed in the secret knock and had the price of the drink.

Our two elderly friends sat quietly in the darkest corner of the bar drinking their half-pints of stout and occasional nips of whiskey. In low tones they plotted the following day's itinerary. If their wren-day peregrinations were to be successful it was imperative that the route they would eventually settle on should be kept secret; hence their isolation and their inaudible murmurings. To be first on the scene was imperative if they were to extract the maximum dues which might quite easily amount to a shilling or even more whereas late arrivals might expect only pence and half-pence and sometimes nothing at all in houses where numerous bands of wren-boys would have already called. All the loose change, so carefully saved for the occasion, would have been expended. Timing, therefore, was of the utmost importance, timing and pacing, the latter meaning that only a limited amount of strong drink should be consumed so that drunkenness be kept at bay at least until the wren-boy itinerary had been completed. Then they would be free to relax in any pub of their choosing for as long as they wished.

For the final time they went over the carefully-laid plans. They proposed to start in the morning, a full hour before first light, to daub their faces, one with black boot polish and the other, for contrast, with brown, then to don their calico suits and caps and finally to shoulder the embroidered green sashes which

97

placed them a cut above the orthodox and the pedestrian. Each would carry an extra pair of shoes or boots strung around the waist to ensure dry and comfortable travel over the twenty miles of town and countryside which they had made their own over two generations. There would be no intoxicating drink until the first half of the journey had been completed but they would breakfast well. They would wrap their instruments in strips of discarded table coverings made from moisture resisting oil cloth. The bodhrán and the concertina need not be utilised, in the event of rain storms, until they found themselves indoors or sheltered by the tall houses of the town. If the weather remained fine they would lighten their journey with lively march tunes. The bodhrán and concertina, always an agreeable and harmonious combination, carried afar to the more isolated homes of the countryside so that the inhabitants thereof would have no trouble identifying the approaching wren-boys and have the appropriate contribution ready. Their plans finalised they sat back on their seats and, being somewhat incapacitated by the mixture of exhaustion, age and liquor, dozed fitfully until a kind neighbour alerted them before closing time and volunteered a lift home in his horse and rail. Both had earlier agreed to spend the night at the abode of the bachelor member of the duo to facilitate early travel. It would not have been the first time that the pair had spent the night together. On special occasions when the intake of drink far exceeded moderation the married member wisely decided to avoid a confrontation with his querulous spouse. Also there was the fact that the same spouse always exercised a poorly-concealed antipathy towards her husband's best friend on the rare occasions when he chose to call to the house on some business or other. Hence her husband's willingness to accept his friend's offer to spend the night. The long hours passed blissfully and from time to time the friends would arise from their comfortable feather beds and sup from the fine stock of beer, wine and spirits which the carefree bachelor had the foresight to install under his own bed and the bed of his friend.

When one would awake at whatever the hour he made sure not to neglect his companion. There would be a tap on the shoulder and a bottle pressed to the lips of the party abed. Before returning to a trouble-free sleep they would sing and reminisce for short periods and then signify with deep, satisfying snores that nature was taking its course.

Then after a particularly long period of sleep both woke at the same time.

'Is that a thrush I hear or is it a blackbird?' the bachelor asked.

'It would seem to me like a blackbird,' came the drowsy response and with that both arose. Only then did they draw the curtains and peer into the darkness of the winter morning. Sure enough, birds everywhere were tuning up for the morning chorus as the darkness began to lighten. Opening the back door of the tiny abode the bachelor cast the waters of the night into a rivulet which flowed cheerily by. Afterwards he peered at the mantelpiece clock in the kitchen and was pleased to see that it still wanted twenty minutes for nine o'clock. He blew on his hands and lighted the bogdeal fire which had been specially set before his excursion to the town on Christmas Day. He applied a lighted match and at once there was a flame of many colours. Swinging the crane around he positioned the bottom of the black kettle above the leaping blaze. Both proceeded with the setting of the table and in this respect their needs were few. In those days side plates were often regarded as the emblems of upstarts and the large tea mugs were never designed to sit comfortably in a saucer. Egg stands were placed at either side of the table in readiness for the two brace of boiled duck eggs which had been lowered in a ladling spoon into the churning bowels of the kettle from the very moment that the first jets of steam came whistling from its spout. Ravenously and speedily they devoured the four boiled duck eggs and with them several mugs of strong tea as well as their fill of bread, butter and jam. It was, after all, Christmas and they were well entitled to jam in addition to the butter. Sated with this sustaining fare they drew on their calico suits and caps. Each placed the traditional sash around the shoulder of the other and applied the facial polish, brown and black. Then they sat for a while humming and didling to themselves as they sorted out their respective repertoires. Then came the first notes of the day and sweet they were, sweet as wild honey the bachelor bodhrán player was quick to admit. 'I declare to God,' said he, 'but that oul' doodle box grows sweeter by the year.' The rehearsal ended, they sloped out into the mild morning. From every bower and bush, bare and all that they were, came the songs and chirpings of a hundred birds. The pair would be cheered along their way by the contributions of thousands more, all eager and willing to extol the benevolent morning.

'We are indeed blessed with the day,' said the bachelor.

'God be praised,' said his friend.

'It could be teeming rain!'

'Or riddled with hail.'

'Or that awful sleet. How would you like that?'

'I wouldn't like it at all' came the reply. With that the bodhrán player struck his drum in thanksgiving and for good measure the concertina launched into a series of rousing marches which would carry them as far as the town's outskirts. No happier pair ever trod the wintry road. No musicians ever revelled more in their vibrant renderings. No marchers ever tripped so lightly despite their ponderous years and no hearts ever beat so hopefully for by all the laws there were good times ahead and better times to follow.

'We're the first thank God,' said one to the other when he saw that no other wren-boy or band of wren-boys had preceded them to the rich, early pickings of suburbia. They decided to serenade the occupants of the imposing edifices at either side of the roadway with tunes of a romantic nature. Having provided a pleasing if short succession of same they waited for the doors to open. They looked upward as they had done for so many years expecting the bedroom windows to be opened and the coins to come cascading down. They were truly perplexed when nothing happened.

'Better knock 'em up and get 'em out of it,' the bodhrán player smote upon his goat-skin drum with clenched fist until the instrument trembled and boomed. The sound would carry through the empty streets and laneways from one end of the town to the other. As he advertised their presence his friend approached the first house and knocked lightly upon the door. It was an imposing residence with that kind of ornamental door which frowns upon loud knocking. After a short while a small, bespectacled boy answered. His mother, clad in dressing-gown and slippers, stood behind him, a confused look upon her kind face. The wren-boys knew her from other years. Always she was worth a shilling or a sixpence depending upon her mood.

'I'm sorry,' she explained, 'but we finished with all that yesterday.' Well used to rebuff the pair moved on to the door of the next house only to be told the same story. Mystified they moved on to the next, now fearing the worst. The priest must have been at it again, turning the people of town and country against wren-boys! Baffled as to why the clergy should have undergone such an unexpected change of heart they decided nevertheless to proceed as planned. They were quickly brought down to earth when the crotchety old pensioner who responded to the irritating doorbell in the next house asked them if they knew the day they had.

Only then did it dawn on the luckless pair that they were a day late. To make doubly sure they asked the old man for a look at the newspaper which he held behind his back.

There it was, as plain as the ribs of the dangling concertina, 27 December 1939. So they were a day late. Little as it was in the calendar of the year it might as well have been six months. Saint Stephen's Day, the day of the wren, the day for which they had planned since the same day the year before had slipped silently by while they drank and slept their fill in the curtained room of the tiny cottage.

'It's a pity we didn't think of drawing the curtains,' said the bodhrán player as he smote his instrument with bent head.

'If only we had taken a look at the clock now and then!' his friend moaned as he extracted a long, mournful note from his concertina. They stood silently side by side looking down at the roadway and tiring of looking down looked upward despairingly at the grey skies still devoid of rain.

'What possessed us at all!' the bodhrán player asked.

'What possessed us but drink!' came the instant answer. As they stood dejectedly not knowing which way to turn the housewives and children of the suburb where they found themselves stood in their doorways and gateways. None smiled at the plight of the elderly pair and there was no laughter, no titter and no guffaw to further confuse the latter-day wren-boys. Rather were their concerned faces tinged with sadness. They were reminded of the errors of age, of fathers and grandfathers once dearly loved but now, alas, gone forever from the scene, gone maybe but recalled for a while by the presence of the ancient pair who had arrived too late. After several uneasy moments the drooping, downcast musicians in their snow-white apparel and peaked caps decided to call it a day but then an odd thing happened. A postman with a bag of New Year cards slung around his neck came cycling past. The reason he had the bag slung around his neck instead of his shoulders was because he had a satchel, with a half dozen of stout inside, slung across his back. Upon beholding the strange pair on the roadway he dismounted.

'Attention!' he called sharply. Immediately the wren-boys sprung to attention. They were, in a sense, uniformed men and was not the man who had barked the order also in uniform. Uniform is as uniform does and those who are bound must obey!

Furthermore; was not this man's uniform provided by the state and was not the state the highest authority. They stood, therefore, awaiting further orders and never, it must be truthfully said, did two out of place, out of time wren-boys need orders so badly.

The postman, wheeling his bicycle at his side, circled the elderly pair as though he were inspecting a guard of honour. He noted the stubble on the jaws and shook his head sadly at such a lapse in standards. He noted the stale odour of intoxicating liquor and the untied flies and the rakish tilt of the caps and the mud on the shoes and all the other things that an old campaigner bemoans as he conducts his tour of inspection.

'At ease!' The order was given in a lighthearted manner and, explicitly, there came across the message that he was, difficult as it might be to believe, once a wren-boy himself. Who was to say, in fact, that he had not arrived late on the scene on some far-off occasion! He made a final circle around the now relaxed wrenboys, hummed and hawed a few times and asked who was the cashier.

The bodhrán player indicated that he filled such a post. Without a word the postman swept the cap from the bodhrán player's head and, allowing his bike to fall to the ground, thrust a hand into his trousers' pocket, located a sixpenny piece and dropped it into the cap. Then he moved among the many women who had gathered to agonise over the plight of the oldsters. Pence, threepenny pieces, sixpenny pieces and even a shilling were willingly contributed before the postman ran out of subscribers.

'Now,' said he as he handed back the jingling cap to its rightful owner, 'you will strike up a tune and you will march proudly with heads held high right into the very heart of the town and remember that a good wren-boy, like a good man, is never late.'

The tune, a rousing one, was forthcoming at once. The wren-boys drew themselves up to their full heights.

'By the left quick march,' came the curt command from the postman. Sprightly and in step the wren-boys marched off in tune with the music.

'Remember,' the postman called after them, 'once a wren-boy always a wren-boy according to the order of MacMoolamawn.'

'The order of MacMoolamawn!' they echoed the name, not knowing that MacMoolamawn was the first wren-boy of all the wren-boys. The postman mounted his bicycle and cycled outward with his bag of letters and satchel of stout.

CIDER

I FORGET MY exact age during the Christmas in question but I must have been at least seventeen for, dare I say it gentle reader, I was greatly addicted to cider and foolishly believed that I could drink any amount of it. Addicted though I was I drank it but rarely and always discreetly. My father had his suspicions but he never caught me in the act and always I made sure to steal into bed when I was intoxicated. With companions of my own age I would indulge in secret sessions on certain feast days and holy days about five times a year in all and once at Christmas. That would have been the Christmas I saw and heard the banshee.

The banshee was heard only when a person with an O or a Mac in the surname passed away. Originally my family were O'Kanes and none was surer than myself that this plaintive and panic-inducing apparition would not be duped by the minor deviation in name.

I had heard the banshee in the past. We would be sitting by the fire late at night, my mother darning socks, my father reading the newspaper of the day and we, the children, readying ourselves for bed.

'Hush!' my mother would suddenly raise a hand for absolute silence. In moments the requisite hush would have descended and then, fully alerted, we would wait for the inevitable with looks of alarm on our faces. From afar would come the supernatural wailing, spine-chilling and pitiful, not belonging to this world. My mother would make the sign of the cross while we all followed suit except my father.

'Another poor soul on its way to the great beyond,' my mother would whisper.

'Another sex-starved greyhound,' my father would announce with a good-humoured shake of his head.

Time rolled on and the family grew. One month I would be five feet six and by the end of the following month I would be five feet seven. It was growing time. By the time Christmas arrived I was five feet ten inches and rapidly heading for six feet.

It had been agreed that my father, my mother and the girls would assemble in the kitchen at eleven-thirty so that all would be in time for Midnight Mass at the church of Saint Mary's. Earlier we had partaken of lemonade and biscuits in honour of the season. After the turkey had been trussed and stuffed in readiness for Christmas Day my father was declared exempt from further involvement in the household chores. He headed at once for the neighbourhood pub where most of his cronies would already have ensconced themselves. For days before I had strenuously argued that I had grown too old to be a part of the familistic excursion to the church reminding my parents of my great age and height and pointing out that all my friends had received permission to attend Mass on their own or with their chosen companions.

My sisters took my part but my father was adamant saying it had come to his ears that the teenagers of the parish were more interested in cider and porter than in the pursuance of their Christmas duties. In the end he relented but only when my mother forcibly reminded him that he had been young himself.

'Very well so,' I remember his words well as he clasped his hands behind his back, 'but if it comes to my attention that you place the consumption of cider before the fulfilment of your religious duties I will confine you to your room for twenty-four hours, without recourse to appeal, and in addition I will kick your posterior so hard that your front teeth will fall out as a result.'

'Cider!' I spat out the word disdainfully as though it were the last thought in my head.

Two hours before midnight I slipped out of the house by the back door and joined my friends in Moorey's public house. The only light in the tiny bar was from a flickering candle. The limbs of the law were abroad on public house duty and Moorey spoke in whispers.

'Happy Christmas!' he said and handed me a pint of cider on the house.

Moorey was old as the hills, grey as a slate, ribald, randy and irreligious but he was a generous soul and no other publican in town would serve us for fear of reprisals from parents and the custodians of the peace. Despite this my mother and the other matrons of the street liked him. They had known his late wife. He had apparently loved her dearly and had always shown it in his treatment of her while she was alive. He had not remarried although she had been dead for thirty years. Every Sunday he would place fresh flowers on her grave. Like ourselves he was addicted to cider with the difference that he would lace his pints with dollops of whiskey and yet we never saw him drunk. Sometimes there would be the barest suggestion of a lurch but nothing remotely resembling the phenomenal staggers executed by seemingly indestructible drunkards when the pubs were closed for the night.

While we sat quietly drinking pint after pint of cider we spoke for the most part about girls, sometimes maliciously and sometimes boastfully which is the way of youth.

As the midnight hour drew near we could hear the hurrying footsteps outside the window as young and old made their way to Midnight Mass. As if by common consent there was no conversation, no laughter, none of the raucous cries one associates with crowds or noisy clatter of boots and shoes. Such was the love and respect for the celebratory season that unnecessary noises were regarded in the same light as profanities.

At ten minutes to twelve Moorey announced that it was time to go. At such an hour, on any other night of the year, the session would only be starting but as

Moorey explained gently: 'Because of the night that's in it boys I think it's time to douse the candle.'

We finished our pints in the pitch dark promising to meet again on Saint Stephen's night. In turn we shook hands with Moorey and extended to him the compliments of season. Outside on the street only the stragglers remained.

We had earlier decided against Mass for a number of reasons; if our parents saw us they would immediately recognise our state of intoxication. Then there was the possibility that one or more of us would be nauseated by the heat of the church and the burning incense, which could well bring on a fit of vomiting. Then there was the most important factor of all and that was the likelihood that one or more of us would be obliged to lessen the strain on brimming bladders and to do this it would be necessary to stand up in the full view of the congregation and make one's way to the end of one's pew and thence up the long aisle under the suspicious stares of friends, neighbours, parents and strangers. Many would smirk knowingly, aware of our plight and destination, which would of necessity be the convenient back wall of the holy sanctuary which was attached to the rear of the church. Our parents, of course, would be infuriated, knowing full well that we would have to be truly cider-smitten to run such a gauntlet!

We went our separate ways with none of the boisterous farewells in which we would indulge on less devotional occasions. At home the kitchen was strangely silent. On the mantelpiece the clock, unheard throughout the day, was having its full say at last. A burned-out turf sod crumbled softly into the overflowing ashpan of the Stanley Number 8.

I suddenly felt a profound longing for the girls and for my parents. Supposing they never came back! I dismissed the terrible thought and counted the twelve intrusions which introduced the midnight hour. The final chime extended itself to the ultimate limits where silence lay waiting to receive its spirit. Then, from the rear of the house, came a long, low, wailing sound which made the hairs stand to attention on that area of the head nearest to my forehead. I had known these hairs all my life and I can swear that they never behaved in such a fashion before. While I waited for them to resume their normal stance there came, stealing through the partly-opened back door of the kitchen, the same wailing sound. My hairs remained alert while my heart raced and my whole frame shivered. Suddenly I grew less tense. This new state was no doubt induced by a mixture of cider and youthful bravado!

The wailing started again, this time more protracted and pitiful, as though the soul of the voice box from which it originated had been recently drowned in the unfathomable depths of black despair.

Again my heart raced and the hairs already standing were joined by their brethren from every quarter of the head. Such was their consistency that they would have served as a bed of nails for a novice fakir. Only the wailing of the banshee could stiffen human hairs to such a degree.

Then, for the first time in my entire life, my knees knocked and I was obliged to place my hands on the table for support. There came almost immediately a sustained high-pitched pillalooing of such intensity that I was obliged to stuff my fingers in my ears lest my hearing be permanently damaged. It was as though the ghostly proprietress of such unearthly vocal organs was endeavouring to reach notes never attained before. Their pitch seemed to far exceed the range of the most accomplished soprano and then, unexpectedly, came a collapsing and a crumbling followed by a mixture of base trebles and last of all by the most musical grunts and groans imaginable as though the banshee in question was about to give birth.

Emboldened by the cider I cautiously made my way into our back yard. The sickle moon shone fitfully, its pale glow frequently impaired by heedless clouds.

Slowly I advanced towards the back door of the out-house where the winter's supply of turf was stored.

I had frequently heard of the silence of the grave when older folk spoke reverently of the dead and such indeed was the silence of the out-house at that point in time on that unforgettable night. I was not prepared for what happened next. I was standing close to the rickety door straining my ears for telltale sounds when I head the uneven breathing of some creature in the immediate vicinity of the door's exterior. On second thoughts, panting might be a more apt word. Then came a horrifying caterwauling as terrifying as it was unexpected. It exploded right into my ear which was pressed against the door. I was paralysed, my feet like hundred-weights of lead, my heart thumping as though, at any minute, it would burst through the walls of my chest. I would have taken off that instant but my legs refused to budge. I was tied down by my own terror. I prayed silently to the Blessed Virgin.

'Mother of the Sacred Jesus,' I whispered imploringly, 'come to my aid this night.'

Suddenly my natural courage, scant as it was, surfaced and with a mighty roar I opened the door. The creature tumbled in on top of me and we both fell in a heap astride the turf sods scattered around the floor. She persisted with her lamentations as she lay on the ground writhing and kicking out in torment.

It was as much as I could do to get to my feet. When I did I fell a second time on top of the black shawled creature from the spirit world. I had accidentally stood on a turf sod which spun beneath my foot, capsizing me. This time I rolled over on my side in a desperate effort to escape the clutches of the hideous creature with the overpowering smell.

At that moment a wayward moon shaft entered the out-house through its only window and highlighted the features of the awful apparition which would surely tear my eyes out if she could but lay her filthy talons on me.

The moon shaft rested for a moment on the blood-shot eyes before drifting downwards to the almost toothless mouth, redeemed from emptiness by the presence of a solitary black fang from which venom dripped as she tried in vain to smite me.

In anguish I cried out to the heavens for help and the heavens in their mercy answered. I dived through the out-house window and into the back yard where my head struck a stone so that I was rendered half unconscious.

Fuming and screaming and uttering unmentionable maledictions she towered over me. A number of small bones materialised in her grimy paws. These she flung at me with all her might but most whizzed harmlessly by. One struck me just above the eye. There was no doubt about its origin. It was a human finger bone as were the others which lay scattered about the back yard.

I managed to crawl away from her towards the door of the kitchen. Curiously she made no attempt to follow me. On all fours, like a wounded animal, I made for the sanctuary of the kitchen.

I bolted the door behind me and ran up the stairs to bed where I pulled the clothes over my head without disrobing. I lay there shaking and moaning, beseeching the Blessed Mother of God to succour and comfort me.

After a while I slunk from the bed to the window which commanded a full view of the back yard and out-house. The moon had just unloaded a cargo of ghastly light. There was no sign of the banshee.

Making the Sign of the Cross I returned to my bed and promptly fell asleep. No doubt the shock of the night's happenings played a part in my sudden collapse into deep slumber. The next sound I heard was my mother's voice calling me in the half light of the morning.

'Hurry!' she was saying, 'and you'll just be on time for ten o'clock Mass.'

I lay on my bed fervently wishing that I had not consumed so much of Moorey's cider. It was only then that the awful happenings of the night came flooding back. I hurried downstairs. My father sat at the head of the table smoking his pipe. He threw me a withering look before the commencement of his interrogation.

Before he had time to pose a single question I blurted out my story. Horrified, my poor mother clutched her bosom and flopped into the chair which my father had instantly provided lest she fall on the floor. As I revealed the full details of my horrific encounter my mother's face grew paler and paler. My father puffed upon his pipe at a furious rate. There was a cloud of blue smoke underhanging the ceiling by the time I finished.

'The banshee you say!' My father emptied the bowl of his pipe into the ash-pan of the Stanley.

'Without question,' I replied as we both waited for my mother to stop shaking her head. The shaking was accompanied by the most holy of spiritual aspirations, all directed upwards in thanksgiving for my salvation.

My father sighed deeply which meant that he was also thinking deeply. Without another word he filled his pipe while I waited for his verdict. There was none forthcoming. Instead he rose without a word and went into the back yard where he spent a considerable time. When he returned his hands were clasped behind his back.

'You say,' he opened, 'that the bones she flung at you were finger bones!'

'Yes,' came my ready answer.

'Human fingers?'

'Yes.'

He took his right hand from behind his back and threw a fistful of small bones on the table.

'These,' he announced solemnly, 'are the very bones which lay scattered around the yard just now. Will you confirm that these are the bones which were flung at you last night by the banshee?'

'There's no doubt in my mind,' I replied.

Guardedly I fingered the bones which still retained some tissue and a residue of meat. It was clear that they had been well and truly gnawed.

'And you say they are human?' My father was now at his most inquisitorial. All the family knew that he secretly fancied himself as a prosecutor. He was always at the head and tail of every domestic investigation, strutting around the kitchen with his hands clasped behind his back, taking them apart occasionally and joining them together at the uppermost point of his paunch as he listened to evidence and submissions.

Sometimes he would close his eyes as he questioned a hostile witness. Other times he would stand silently for long periods, his eyes firmly fixed upon the defendant who was generally myself. This tactic nearly always worked with the girls who would readily confess to anything, just to be free of his accusing eye. I must say that the entire household enjoyed such trials at the end of which everybody, except yours truly, was acquitted and exonerated. When convicted I would be confined to my bedroom for periods of one hour to a maximum of four although the possibility of a twenty-four hour sentence was always on the cards.

'My Lord!' he unexpectedly addressed himself to my mother who had sufficiently recovered her composure to acknowledge the surprise judicial appointment, 'these bones you see before you which the defendant claims are human finger bones are nothing of the sort. They are, in fact, bones from a pig's foot or crubín which is the local term affectionately applied to this particular extension of the pig's anatomy.'

My mother rose to examine the evidence, nodded her head in agreement and resumed her seat.

'Not only is the defendant a pathological liar,' my father was continuing, 'but he is a deceitful scoundrel as well.'

'Please proceed!' was all my mother said.

113

My father cleared his throat.

'You are aware,' said he, 'of the existence of a woman known as Madgeen Buggerworth?'

'Yes!' I replied with a laugh.

'You will respect the court sir!' my father cautioned, 'or you'll be fined for contempt.'

I bent my head submissively and tried to look contrite. This wasn't easy for the very mention of Madgeen Buggerworth's name was enough to make anyone laugh. She was a local begger-woman and it was frequently said of her that she never drew a sober breath. On reflection it would be true to say that I had never seen her sober.

Madgeen was a powerful virago of a woman. Her husband had died after siring the final member of her thirteen strong family and the family, the moment they were fledged, took off for foreign parts and were never seen again and small blame to them because she was never done with scolding and beating them.

Her favourite pose was when she spread her legs apart in the middle of the roadway and threw off the black shawl which truly covered multitudes. Up then would go the front of her skirts so that her bare midriff was exposed to the world. Then would come the drunken boast as she touched her navel with the index finger of her right hand: 'There now,' she would call out at the top of her voice for all to hear, 'there now is a belly that never reared a bastard!'

She would rant and rave, skirts aloft until the civic guards came on the scene and ushered her homewards. Other times she was to be seen lying in one of the town's laneways with her back to a wall, fast asleep, snoring in drunken abandon. Given enough drink she could sleep anywhere, regardless of wind or rain. She was to be seen too late at night staggering from one doorway to another singing at the top of her voice if singing it could be called.

'If it please the court I would request that your worship and the defendant follow me to the out-house where I shall provide incontrovertible evidence that this man,' my father pointed a finger in my direction, 'was so bereft of sense from the consumption of cider that he confused our friend Madgeen Buggerworth with the banshee.'

He led the way into the back yard and on to the out-house where we were greeted by deep snoring punctuated now and then by outbreaks of spluttering and wheezing. There on the ground, partly covered by turf sods, lay Madgeen Buggerworth. By her side there lay an uneaten crubín.

'We'll let her sleep for the present,' my father announced, 'later,' again he pointed in my direction, 'when she wakes you will serve her with dinner and afterwards you will take her home.'

I hoped that this would be his last word on the matter but there was more to follow.

'Let us return to the kitchen,' he said solemnly, 'where your sentence will be handed down. Meanwhile I suggest you pray for mercy.'

So saying he preceded us into the kitchen where he announced that he was relieving my mother of all judicial responsibilities on the grounds that she would be incapable because of her known affection for the defendant of meting out a just sentence.

I stood with my back to the Stanley awaiting the pleasure of the court. My father stood at the doorway, hands clasped behind back. My mother sat in a neutral corner.

'I find you guilty of drunkenness in the first degree,' he said, 'and I hereby sentence you to twenty-four hours solitary confinement in your room.'

I stood aghast! It was the toughest sentence he had ever handed down. I would have to admit that I expected no less. He was clearing his throat again.

'There are, however,' he proceeded solemnly, 'mitigating circumstances. This day as you know is the birthday of a great and good man who was once wrongly convicted and subsequently crucified. As a small measure of atonement for that woeful miscarriage of justice I hereby suspend the sentence imposed upon you. You are, therefore, entitled to walk from this court a free man.'

On my way home from Mass I met him walking down the street against me. It had turned unexpectedly into the mildest of days.

'Let's have a stroll before dinner,' he suggested.

We took the pathway to the river which was in modest flood. He spoke about other Christmases, of his father and grandfather and of great wobbling geese especially stall fed for the Christmas dinner, of whiskey drinking, great-uncles and carol singing and the innocent pranks of his youth. We walked through the oak wood, marvelling at the splendid contributions of the songbirds despite the greyness of the day and the leafless trees and hedgerows.

We re-entered the town at the end farthest from where we left it and proceeded down the long thoroughfare known as Church Street. We turned off into a laneway and found ourselves at the rear door of Moorey's premises. I was astonished to discover that my father was familiar with the sesame of admission, two knocks and a pause, two knocks a pause and finally three knocks. The door opened after a short wait and Moorey stood there, surprise showing on his face.

'Long time no see, Master!' he said with a smile.

Inside we sat on stools at the bar counter.

'Do you think this man has graduated from cider Moorey?' my father asked.

Moorey considered the question carefully before answering. Then after a while he said: 'Just about.'

'Then,' said my father as he laid a hand on my shoulder, 'we'll have two pints of stout to sharpen the appetite.'

MANY YEARS AGO

MANY YEARS AGO, in our street, there lived an old woman who had but one son whose name was Jack. Jack's father had died when Jack was no more than a garsún but Jack's mother went out to work to support her son and herself.

As Jack grew older she still went out and worked for the good reason that Jack did not like work. The people in the street used to say that Jack was only good for three things. He was good for eating, he was good for smoking and he was good for drinking. Now to give him his due he never beat his mother or abused her verbally. All he did was to skedaddle to England when she was too old to go out to work. Years passed but she never had a line from her only son. Every Christmas she would stand inside her window waiting for a card or a letter. She waited in vain.

When Christmas came to our street it came with a loud laugh and an expansive humour that healed old wounds and lifted the hearts of young and old. If the Christmas that came to our street were a person he would be something like this: he would be in his sixties but glowing with rude health. His face would be flushed and chubby with sideburns down to the rims of his jaws. He would be wearing gaiters and a bright tweed suit and he would be mildly intoxicated. His pockets would be filled with silver coins for small boys and girls and for the older folk he would have a party at which he would preside with his waist-coated paunch extending benignly and his posterior benefiting from the glow of a roaring log fire.

There would be scalding punch for everybody and there would be roast geese and ducks, their beautiful golden symmetries exposed in large dishes and tantalising gobs of potato-stuffing oozing and bursting from their rear-end stitches. There would be singing and storytelling and laughter and perhaps a tear here and there when absent friends were toasted. There would be gifts for everybody and there would be great good will as neighbours embraced, promising to cherish each other truly till another twelve months had passed.

However, Christmas is an occasion and not a person. A person can do things, change things, create things but all our occasions are only what we want them to be. For this reason Jack's mother waited, Christmas after Christmas, for word of her wandering boy. To other houses would come stout registered envelopes from distant loved ones who remembered. There would be bristling, crumply, envelopes from America with noble rectangular cheques and crisp, clean, dollars to delight the eye and comfort the soul. There would be parcels and packages of all shapes and sizes so that every house became a warehouse until the great day came when all goods would be distributed.

Now it happened that in our street there was a postman who knew a lot more about its residents than they knew about themselves. When Christmas came he was weighted with bags of letters and parcels. People awaited his arrival the way children awaited a bishop on confirmation day. He was not averse to indulging in a drop of the comforts wherever such comforts were tendered but comforts or no the man was always sensitive to the needs of others. In his heart resided the spirit of Christmas. Whenever he came to the house where the old woman lived he would crawl on all fours past the windows. He just didn't have the heart to go by and be seen by her. He hated to disappoint people, particularly old people. For the whole week before Christmas she would take up her position behind the faded curtains, waiting for the letter which

118

never came.

Finally the postman could bear it no longer. On Christmas Eve he delivered to our house a mixed bunch of cards and letters. Some were from England. He requested one of these envelopes when its contents were removed. He rewrote the name and address and also he wrote a short note which he signed 'your loving son Jack'. Then from his pocket he extracted a ten shilling note, a considerable sum in those far-off days. He placed the note in the envelope. There was no fear the old woman would notice the handwriting because if Jack was good at some things, as I have already mentioned, he was not good at other things and one of these was writing. In fact, Jack could not write his own name. When the postman came to the old woman's door he knocked loudly. When she appeared he put on his best official voice and said: 'Sign for this if you please Missus.'

The old woman signed and opened the envelope. The tears appeared in her eyes and she cried out loud:

'I declare to God but Jack is a scholar.'

'True for you,' said the postman, 'and I daresay he couldn't get in touch with you until he learned to write.'

'I always knew there was good in him,' she said. 'I always knew it.'

'There's good in everyone Missus,' said the postman as he moved on to the next house.

The street was not slow in getting the message and in the next and last post there were many parcels for the old woman. It was probably the best Christmas the street ever had.

A CHRISTMAS
PERFORMANCE

HECTOR FITZPITTER, PLAYER-manager-author, sat on his trunk. It was his only possession apart from his hat, suit, shirt and the shoes in which he stood. He had been sitting in the same position for an hour and a half. Occasionally he made a slight concession to ache and cramp by gently lifting and relocating his numb buttocks slightly because the shiny, well-worn seat of his trousers was beginning to fray and might not survive a more energetic adjustment. The last of his coins had been expended earlier in the day on a cup of tea and a cheese sandwich.

'You don't have enough for ham,' the restaurant owner had cautioned after he had calculated the pennies, halfpennies and solitary sixpenny piece which Hector had extravagantly spread across the counter top.

'What have I enough for then?' he had asked petulantly.

'Cheese sandwich,' came the disinterested reply, 'and even then you're short.'

Hector pretended he hadn't heard, secretly hoping that the sandwich and tea would be forthcoming without further reference to financial discrepancy. The chest on which he sat contained his costumes, tattered and torn and sadly reduced to three in number, Iago, Falstaff and Tontagio, in the *Bearded Monster of Tontagio*, the eponymous role for which he was best known and indeed revered in smaller towns and villages. It was a fearsome part which left unsophisticated audiences cowering and abject as he ranted and raved all over the stage, directing his more savage

120

outbursts towards the meeker-looking members of the audience who faithfully responded with screams and fainting fits.

He had written the play himself. Once, in his heyday, he had fallen through a trapdoor. He had broken a leg and had penned the piece during the subsequent six weeks of hospitalisation and convalescence.

'Would,' said a particularly scurrilous provincial critic, 'that he had broken his hand instead of his leg and spared us this infantile gibberish!'

Another called him the clown prince of balderdash and compared him with the village idiot on one of his worse days. The cruelest came from an amateur actor who wrote a weekly theatre column and who lambasted all visiting plays and players with unrefined vitriol and without exception, reserving his more generous encomiums for the annual offering of the local amateur drama group of which he was a member.

Said he; 'Not satisfied with the immortal roles created by Shakespeare, Sheridan, O'Neill, etcetera, Fitzpitter dives deep into his psyche and surfaces covered in his own crud.'

Another wrote that Herbert Fitzpitter should be hung drawn and quartered, 'hung,' he suggested, 'for directing the play, drawn for taking the leading role and quartered for writing the damned thing!'

Hector Fitzpitter revelled in such notices, attributing the lack of appreciation to ignorance and jealousy. Now, virtually at the end of his career, his unpaid company scattered to the four winds and his pockets empty he would surely have wept had it not been for the fact that he had never shed a genuine tear since he first embarked on an acting career at the tender age of seventeen, all of fifty years before his present predicament. A lesser man would have despaired and thrown himself at the mercy of the county.

For Hector Fitzpitter his present plight was merely a temporary reversal, a minor stumbling-block on the long road to the recognition which surely lay around the corner. Meanwhile there was the question of board and lodgings. His leading lady and his several underlings knew how to look after themselves. They would regroup instinctively, aided by the theatre grapevine, at a specific venue during the first days of spring. All save he were now gone to ground in their own homes or other safe havens for the Christmas which was almost upon them. The spiritual balm of the season would quickly heal the trauma which they had all endured when the *Bearded Monster of Tontagio* closed prematurely. The proprietor of the theatre had confiscated the slender takings of the three nights before it folded, pointing out to Hector that the paltry amount would hardly pay for the electricity not to mention himself, the caretaker, the box-office staff, the cleaners and the general upkeep.

Wearily, Hector Fitzpitter rose to his feet. He shivered as the north-eastern gusts reminded him that he should not have pawned his overcoat. Cutting as the gusts were they were not as damaging as the review of a local amateur.

'The audience,' wrote he, 'few as they were from front seat to back, were soon drenched by the spume and spittle which accompanied the uncontrolled rantings of Mr Hector Fitzpitter.'

There had been more but Hector had not read on. Attacking an actor over the incidental discharge of a minute particle of saliva was akin to criticising a person for having a hump or a stammer. It just wasn't done. He walked slowly down the street, dragging the cumbersome trunk behind him. Time was when he would have effortlessly borne it on his shoulder.

Hector Fitzpitter was possessed of a large and ungainly frame. The excess flesh which once rippled on his torso now shuddered and trembled like a blancmange at the least exertion. He presented a formidable figure to those who encountered him for the first time. Younger actors feared him not at all.

'Blubber!' they would reply contemptuously when

asked if the outsize player-manager-author might not be a dangerous adversary in a confrontation. Elaborating, they would explain that he was never less than a dangerous antagonist on the stage and finding himself with a naked sword in his hand was quite capable of slashing at anything that got in his way. Similarly when fisticuffs were demanded during a violent scene he was apparently the equivalent of a Jack Johnson and often knocked down younger opponents as though they were made of straw.

'But,' they would be quick to explain, 'in real life he is a cowardly wretch who wouldn't fight to save his life.'

'In fact,' one of Hector's closest friends informed a curious reporter, 'while the fellow would not hesitate for a moment to save a damsel in distress on the stage he would run a mile if called upon to do so in public.'

After several hundred yards of trudging he found himself at the front door of the lodgings which he had vacated that morning, having met half of his obligations before saying farewell and promising to pay the other half when funds came to hand as he put it to Mrs Melrick the accommodating landlady who tired easily of his many long-winded apologists.

She was anything but receptive to his second proposal of the day, board and lodgings until his ship came in. Rather curtly she pointed out that all of her lodgers without exception would be returning to their various homes for Christmas and since she expected to find herself with an empty house throughout Christmas Eve, Christmas Day and the three days following, she had decided to stay with her son and daughter-in-law in a nearby town for the period of the closure.

'I'm doing it for my son and grandson,' she explained to Hector, despondent of face, his jaws resting on intertwined hands atop his now vertical trunk. His thoughts were elsewhere, his attention diverted to the unlikely prospect of alternative accommodation. The thought of sleeping out was an appalling one. He had

123

resorted to it on occasion in his younger days and then only in summer time. At his present age and in winter time it would have been suicidal. His ears pricked suddenly when she referred to her daughter-in-law directly for the first time.

'Bitch!' she was saying.

Her remarks were not addressed altogether to Hector. Ruefully she recalled, for her own benefit, the inexplicable antics and tantrums of her son's wife. From what he heard it was not difficult to gather that there was bad blood between mother-in-law and daughter-in-law.

'It beats me,' Hector Fitzpitter cut across her ill-concealed disgruntlement, 'how you've endured it for so long.'

'God alone knows that,' she replied vigorously, roused to full articulation by the obviously sincere commiseration from this unexpected quarter.

'You know about her?' Mrs Melrick asked.

'Who doesn't!' came the ready reply.

'She's something isn't she?'

Hector Fitzpitter thought for a moment before responding.

'She's might pull the wool over my son's eyes,' the landlady warmed to her task, 'but she won't pull it over mine!'

'She's not worth it,' Hector shook his head secondly. A great sorrow clouded his face.

'She's not fit to polish your shoes,' he continued as Mrs Melrick opened the door wide so that he might follow her, trunk and all, into the kitchen. Over the tea which followed they spoke at length about the wickedness and countless misdeeds of her son's wife. To add criminality to her natural sinfulness there was confirmation also that the awful creature was pregnant again.

'What next!' Hector asked as he lifted his eyes to heaven. He was enjoying the role no end. What a pity that playwrights, royalty-hungry, so-called moderns, could not write such parts! The exchanges between the pair lasted until the first of the boarders arrived for the evening meal.

'See out there,' Mrs Melrick pointed out the kitchen window to a tiny annex, erected by her late husband for their only son as a facility for his studies.

'You can stay there until my return,' his benefactress informed him. 'There's a divan and I'll leave in a few blankets. You can eat here tonight and tomorrow night but after I've left you must fend for yourself. You must not come near the house.'

There had been other conditions but, by and large, Hector felt that he had not been mistreated. The following day he would enquire as to the whereabouts of the local presbytery. He had always found, so long as one didn't overdo it, that Presbyterians were a most reliable source of food and small amounts of cash and, surely if they had been supportive in the past on everyday occasions, was it not likely that they would be even more charitable at Christmas!

Father Alphonsus Murphy had once seen Hector Fitzpitter on the stage. He had been holidaying at the time in a nearby seaside resort and finding himself with nothing better to do forked out a florin he could ill afford to see the great man's version of Iago. He had intended after the holiday, to repair to the diocesan retreat house for a few days' meditation and a subsequent revelation of his transgressions, minor and all that they were, but decided against it after he had endured two and three-quarter hours in the stuffy marquee which Hector Fitzpitter had rented for the season

'I felt,' he confided to one of his curates some time later, 'that my experience in that marquee was sufficient atonement for anything I might have done since my last visit to the retreat house.'

'Allow me to introduce myself,' Hector Fitzpitter opened rather grandly.

'No need. No need!' Father Murphy put him at his ease.

'Perhaps you've seen me on the stage Father?'

Father Murphy decided to ignore the question. Instead he asked if he might be of some assistance to his urbane visitor.

'You can indeed Father,' came the deferential reply.

After providing a résumé of his recent misfortunes in a style not unfamiliar to his listener, Hector asked if it might be possible to borrow a modest sum of money, to be repaid in full, without fail as soon as the touring season commenced in the forthcoming spring.

'We are not in the business of lending,' Father Murphy reminded him, 'but if you are not averse to a day's work I can provide same and pay you when the job is done.'

'Work!' Hector recoiled instinctively as images of shovel and pick-axes assailed him.

'Don't be alarmed,' Father Murphy had experienced countless reactions of a similar nature. 'Your qualifications for the sort of work I have in mind are impeccable. In fact, I know of nobody off-hand who could do a better job.'

'You want me to read the lesson,' Hector's face beamed as he saw himself addressing a record audience and, more importantly, a captive audience. Father Murphy scowled uncharacteristically at the awful prospect.

'I merely want you,' he said icily, 'to play the role of Santa Claus tomorrow night. I will supply you with hat, beard and coat. After you've eaten I will take you, in advance, to the laneway where you will be delivering gifts to the underprivileged children of the parish.'

Hector smiled. The prospect appealed to him.

'And I will be paid?'

'Yes,' Father Murphy assured him. 'You will be paid the moment you finish your rounds. Now you may go around the back and tell the housekeeper that I said you were to be fed. I'll expect you to present yourself here tomorrow night at eight o'clock.'

Later, as they drove slowly up the laneway which

126

ended in the open countryside, Father Murphy handed him a pencil and some paper with instructions to write down the name of the owner of each house so that there would be no instances of wrong delivery. Each parcel of gifts would bear the name of the recipient on the outside. By the simple expedient of requesting the house-owner's name the parcels would find their way into the right hands.

'Let me warn you,' Father Murphy's voice assumed a cautionary tone, 'in the very last house you are likely to meet with trouble so you would be best advised not to enter. When your knock is answered you will hand over the gifts to whatever person opens the door. Then, if you have any sense, you will make yourself scarce!'

'You're not trying to tell me that my life will be in danger Father?'

'Not your life,' Father Murphy forced a laugh, 'but the fact is that the parish's biggest bully and its most foul-mouthed drunkard, one Jack Scalp, lives in that house and if he happens to be at home when you call he will most certainly attempt to assault you. By not entering the house you will be in no danger whatsoever. Just turn and leave when your job is done and here,' said Father Murphy, 'is a half-crown. It's Christmas time and you could do with a drink, I daresay, only don't let me see you with a sign of drink on you tomorrow night or I'll clear you from the door!'

Hector Fitzpitter sat upright in the car, a look of affront on his face.

'My dear Father Murphy,' said he, 'I have never drunk before a performance and I don't propose to start now.'

That night Hector slept soundly. He spent most of the following day walking up and down the laneway rehearsing his lines and his movements. He would have been happier with a dress rehearsal but given the circumstances he realised it would be out of the question. During his travels he kept an eye out for Jack Scalp. He had already developed a mental picture of the scoundrel and felt that he would instantly recognise him should their paths cross. He had made up his mind to ignore Father Murphy's warning and was determined to force his way into the kitchen if necessary. If needs be he would exercise his acting skills to their fullest. They had saved him in the past and, with simple presence of mind, would do so again. He drank not at all on Christmas Eve, resolving to splurge on a bellyful of booze as soon as he received his wages. He ate sparingly from the few provisions which Mrs Melrick had left out for him on the wickerwork table in the annex. He made a final inspection of the laneway before calling to the presbytery where Father Murphy awaited him.

'It's a pretty large bag as you can see,' the cleric advised him, 'and there are thirteen households in all. Tarry awhile in the kitchen of each before passing on to the next and take special care at the thirteenth for it is there, as I have told you, that Jack Scalp resides.'

'I'll take care,' Hector promised. If Father Murphy had noticed the contemptuous note in his voice he kept it to himself.

'I will drive you as far as the entrance to the laneway,' he told Hector. He stood by fingering his chin while his protégé fitted the false off-white beard. An elastic band held it firmly in place. Next came the boots which were a size too large but better too large than too small he thought. Then came the hat and finally the long red coat which reached down to his toes.

'Is there a life-size mirror?'

''Fraid not,' Father told him, 'we don't indulge in such vanities in this presbytery but you can take it from me that you look the part.'

Father Murphy wondered if he should inform him of the incident which occurred on the previous Christmas Eve but decided against it. He had already told him to be on his guard. Anyway no great damage had been done, just a bloody nose and that had stopped bleeding after a few moments. The elderly member of the Saint Vincent de Paul Society who had filled the role at the time had been drinking all afternoon and when he pushed Mrs Scalp aside in order to confront her husband he realised that he had bitten off more than he could chew. A string of expletives directed towards him had the effect of momentarily paralysing him. He immediately dropped his bag and made for the door. In vain did Mrs Scalp try to restrain her drunken husband. He knocked her to the floor and landed a solid punch on the somewhat outsize, puce-coloured proboscis of Father Christmas. The blow might have been followed by another but Jack Scalp tripped across a beer crate and fell in a heap on the floor. His intended victim emitted a cry of relief and never drew breath until he arrived at the presbytery, his artificial beard well and truly bloodied. He collapsed onto a chair, gasping for whiskey. His account of the incident differed greatly from the actual facts. He had, according to himself, fought a heroic fight and was forced to retreat lest he do further damage and maybe even be the cause of widowing poor Mrs Scalp who was fully exonerated for not taking sides.

Hector Fitzpitter was rapturously received by the parents and children in the first house he entered. Whiskey and wine were pressed upon him so that he found himself unable to resist. It was the same at all the other homes. His best efforts to refuse the liquor which was so generously pressed upon him were to no avail. Glass after glass of whiskey found its way to his palate and later to his brain. He was, as he would say later, almost suffocated with alcohol.

'You're a big, brave man,' one poor woman had said to him, 'what's a little drop of drink to you?'

He was never possessed of the mettle to refuse drink when kindly souls insisted he partake. In one house a selection of sandwiches awaited him and in another a plate of crackers and cheddar. 'The poor are so open-hearted,' he would say later to Father Murphy, 'they would give you their hearts.'

Father Murphy concurred. He had more than adequate proof of the veracity of Hector Fitzpitter's conclusions.

Children sat on Hector's lap and plied him with dainties. A few days' hence and the cupboards would be bare once more all along the little laneway but here was Christmas and it was a time for giving and no better man to receive than this outstanding representation of Santa Claus, undoubtedly the most colourful ever to visit the laneway. Hector was quite overcome in the face of such bounty, such cordiality, such love! In some of the houses there were sessions of hymn-singing and in others storytelling. Hector Fitzpitter never played so many roles in so short a time.

It was well on the road to midnight when he reached the last house. Drunk as he was he had not forgotten Father Murphy's warning. He drew himself up to his full height. He had played a bear once in *A Winter's Tale* and for a moment was tempted to roar like one. He resisted the urge and gently knocked at the door. None came to answer. He listened for a while but could hear nothing. He knelt and placed an ear against the keyhole. After a short spell there came the most unpropitious sounds. No actor, he told himself, could create such heart-rending whimperings. Faint and childlike, they seemed to emanate from the very depths of human despair. Hardened as he was Hector Fitzpitter found himself physically bereft of strength so moved was he by the broken whinings, eerie and awesome. They succeeded in transmitting a devastating anguish to his heart, an anguish that he had never before experienced. The salt tears coursed down his face and into his adopted beard as he silently rose to his feet determined to put an end to the pitiful ejaculations which so provoked his newly-found humanity.

He knocked loudly upon the door and, upon receiving no response knocked as loudly as his clenched fists would allow. It was opened by a child, a tear-stained, grimy, undernourished little girl who looked at him with wonder-filled eyes. Behind her stood an equally famished little boy and then, suddenly, there were four more boys and girls, so obviously neglected and deprived, so stunted and wan of face that they looked as if they were all the same age.

'It's Santa Claus,' one whispered. Then in subdued confirmation all mentioned the name revered by children everywhere.

Cautiously Hector Fitzpitter made his way into the kitchen. There was little light save that shed by a paraffin lamp with its wick turned down almost fully. There was no trace of a fire although the night was cold. There was no sign of the mother. The father, Jack Scalp, sat in a corner, his legs stretched in front of him, empty beer bottles all around and a partly filled noggin of whiskey clutched in one of his grimy hands. He snored fitfully. The little girl who had opened the door pressed a finger to her lips entreating silence from the visitor.

'Where is your mother?' Hector asked in a whisper.

'He put her out.' Every one of the six pointed a finger at their sleeping father.

'Why?' Hector asked.

'No why,' the girl who had opened the door replied.

'He does it all the time,' another whispered.

'If he wakes he'll beat us again,' said another still.

'For no reason of course?' Hector suggested. A chorus of affirmative whispers greeted his question.

'I have presents for everybody,' he informed the delighted children. How their faces transformed at the news.

'How little it takes,' Hector told himself between sobs and sighs, 'to please a child!'

He looked from one to the other of the angelic faces and was appalled by the bruises and bloodstains thereon. Hector Fitzpitter would never have the slightest compunction about kicking a fellow-thespian in the rear or socking him one to the jaw but to molest a

131

child in such a fashion smacked of base cowardice and naked savagery.

'Your deliverance is at hand,' he announced solemnly to the children, now making not the least effort to lower his tone. He gathered them round him, quite overcome by the angelic radiance of their faces.

'I want you,' Hector informed them as he allowed his hands to linger on each individual head and face, 'to go and find your mother. I want you to bring her here no matter how she protests. Tell her that it was I, Santa Claus, who sent you. Go now.'

In a flash the children departed.

'Now my fine fellow,' Hector addressed the snorting drunkard in the corner, 'let us determine the quality of thy kidney. Awake fellow!' he bawled, 'awake to meet thy just deserts for as sure as there are stars in the heavens outside justice will be done in this house. Awake lout!' He roared at the top of his voice.

Blearily, angrily, torrents of the vilest curses exploding from his beer-stained mouth, Jack Scalp struggled to his feet. Upon beholding Santa Claus and nobody else he squeezed upon his whiskey noggin and would have smashed it against Hector's head had not the actor seized the hand that would smite him and brought its owner to his knees. Possessed of hitherto untapped strength Hector Fitzpitter seized Jack Scalp by the throat and lifted him to his feet.

'My strength is as the strength of ten,' he roared quoting Tennyson, 'because my heart is pure.'

For the first time in his life Jack Scalp started to experience real fear. That he was in the presence of a madman he had absolutely no doubt. Hector flung him violently into the corner he had just vacated and stomped around the kitchen like one berserk. Suddenly he stopped.

'Do you know me?' he asked the cowering figure, askew in his corner.

Fearfully Jack Scalp shook head. He would have taken flight but that he was paralysed with fear.

132

'I,' said Hector Fitzpitter, 'am the Bearded Monster of Tontagio. I have killed seventeen men in my time and maimed a hundred others. Make your peace with God while you may, you scurvy wretch lest I send you to your maker this instant.'

So saying Hector entered fully into the role he had created and played a thousand times. He stalked round the kitchen, striking further terror into his victim with maniacal roars of laughter.

'Rise!' he commanded. Jack Scalp staggered to his feet, drooling now, certain that his demise was at hand. From an inside pocket in the great red coat Hector withdrew Mrs Melrick's turf-shed hatchet and flung it at the cowering creature in the corner, making sure that he barely missed his head. Then seizing him by the throat he spread-eagled him across the kitchen table and choked him to within a breath of suffocation until the table collapsed beneath the squirming, wriggling child-beater.

Hector lifted him to his feet and slapped his face several times before seizing him by the throat yet again. Red froth bubbled from the monster's mouth as he applied the pressure to his victim's throat. Hector had bitten his tongue, just enough to assure that his spittle would be suitable coloured. Once again he flung the drooling drunkard to one side before presenting another terrifying facet of the monster's make-up. He started to smite upon his chest as though he were a gorilla. The grunting and screeching, the hysterical jabbering and high-pitched screaming which accompanied these most recent gestures were diabolical in the extreme. Jack Scalp fainted.

'Awake villain!' Hector Fitzpitter roared, 'awake to thy fate!'

With that he poured the remains of the abandoned whiskey noggin over the prostrate drunkard's face. Stuttering and begging forgiveness Jack Scalp crawled cravenly around the kitchen, sometimes seizing the trouser legs of his tormentor as he begged for mercy.

'I am tempted to kill you,' Hector spoke in what he believed were spine-chilling tones, the same tones that had sent faint-hearted rustics scampering for the exits before the enactment of another gruesome murder on the stage.

'Spare me. Spare me!' Jack Scalp screamed. 'Spare me and I will change my ways.'

'On your knees then,' Hector stood by with hands behind his back.

'Say after me,' he commanded, 'I will never from this moment forth molest my wife or children again.'

He waited as Jack Scalp repeated the words.

'I will never,' Hector continued, 'to the day I die, taste an intoxicating drink. I will be a model husband and father and I will devote the remainder of my life to the welfare of my children.'

'If you fail to honour your promises on this most sacred of nights I, the Monster of Tantagio will return.' Hector's ominous tones were terrifying in the extreme, 'and I will split you right down the middle with this hatchet I hold in my hand.'

Silently Hector Fitzpitter lifted his empty sack and disappeared into the night. There was no applause, no standing ovation, no cries of author! Yet Hector Fitzpitter knew in his heart of hearts that he had given the finest performance of his career. Actors are never fully satisfied, no more than playwrights are after a play has been performed but Hector had accomplished what all actors aspire to and few achieve. He had given the perfect performance. It mattered not that there was no audience and that there were no critics. He had fulfilled his lifelong dream and developments thereafter would prove him right. Early on the morning of Christmas Day, Jack Scalp presented himself to Father Murphy and took a lifetime pledge against intoxicating drink. It was a pledge he would keep. Never again would he spit at, shout at or molest in any way whatsoever, his long-suffering wife and family. He turned into a model father and became one of the parish's

most respected figures. Hector Fitzpitter's acting improved. He benefited greatly from his performance at
the abode of Jack Scalp. During the following summer
a new version of his masterpiece was warmly received
by audiences and critics alike.

CONSCIENCE MONEY

THE TWINS MICKELOW, Patcheen and Pius, were lookalikes, proportionately built, robust and round and standing at five feet two inches in their stockinged feet.

'They don't chase work,' their parish priest Canon Mulgrave confided to a new Curate, 'but they won't avoid it either so that you couldn't very well call them ne'er do wells.'

'Would you call them easy-going then?' the Curate had suggested respectfully.

'Yes,' the Canon conceded after some consideration, 'easy-going would be a fair characterisation.'

For the most part the twins worked for local farmers on a temporary basis. They were paid at the going rate at the end of each day. These modest but undisclosed earnings were supplemented by the weekly dole which the state provided all the year round.

By parochial standards the twins Mickelow would be classified as comfortable. They also had a cow. She provided milk and, as a consequence, sufficient butter for their needs.

The cow grazed throughout most of the spring, summer and autumn in the one acre haggard at the rear of the house. In the winter she was transferred to the Long Acre except in the direst circumstances when the weather became unbearable when she would be temporarily housed with a limited supply of fodder. On the Long Acre which in this instance extended to the nearest crossroads at either side of the house her search for grass would be supervised by one of the brothers. There was always the danger that in her eagerness to locate choice pickings she would overreach herself and end up in one of the roadside dykes, very often filled with water during the months of January and February. Sometimes in areas of high risk she would be tethered as she sought sustenance beneath the bare hedgerows which sheltered the grassy margins of the narrow roadway.

In many ways the twins enjoyed an idyllic existence untroubled by strife or want. A small garden, sheltered from the prevailing wind by a narrow stand of Sitkas, provided potatoes and the more common vegetables such as turnip and cabbage. A latticed hencoop overhung the wall above the front door in the kitchen and a sturdy hen-house of the lean-to variety rested against the rear of the house next to the back door. It had successfully resisted countless incursions from fox and otter since its erection. There were surplus eggs throughout most of the year and these could be exchanged for provisions when the itinerant egg buyer made his weekly call. Gentle and mild-mannered the twins seldom or ever entertained conflicting opinions. Among strangers they were deferential and meek unless drawn into conversation. Even among those they knew they would be the last to initiate any form of communication.

Fuel for their fires was to be found in abundance in the adjacent bogland where they enjoyed turbary rights for generations. The quality was excellent and a small extra rick was held over until the week before Christmas when it would be disposed of to a local buyer who sold lorry loads to customers in the nearest town.

On Friday nights and Sunday nights they would unfailingly make their companionable way to the crossroads public house which was situated a little over a mile from their thatched abode. Arriving at nine they would depart at twelve. Four pints of stout was their nightly intake. Neither smoked or gambled. Neither paid court to females or fornicated in any way and neither visited the nearest town which nestled comfortably at the centre of a large fertile valley fifteen miles distant over dirt roads and tar roads. As a result they were never short of the wherewithal to indulge their crossroads excursions provided, they often reminded each other, that they stayed within the constraints agreed by themselves. These self-imposed limitations ordained that they attach themselves to no company other than their own. However if a drink chanced to come their way from some drunken or other well-meaning benefactor they allowed themselves the liberty to accept so long as it was clearly understood that nothing was to be expected in return.

There were always bountiful times in the height of summer when Yanks and English exiles came home on holiday. Then the drink would flow freely and there would be morning hangovers but nothing else and by this was meant, as far as the twins Mickelow were concerned, that there a had been no extra financial outlay.

Those who came from England in particular spent heedlessly until all their hard-earned money was gone and they were obliged to return to the construction sites where abundant overtime had helped to finance the holiday in the first place. Full credit to them, they never mourned after their vanished earnings nor did they expect anything in return for their profligacy. They seem resigned, even content in themselves that their pockets were empty.

The twins had often been tempted to call a drink for their one time benefactors, now possessed of nothing save a return ticket, but after weighing the merits and demerits thought better of it and resigned themselves to the prevailing attitude that such misplaced kindness might only result in a demeaning postponement of the exile's departure.

There had, in fact, been at least one occasion when the exile had remained behind as a result of not one but several acts of misplaced charity. After a week he became a travesty of the carefree holidaymaker who had breezed in the door a few short weeks before. Eventually for his own good he was frozen out and, all too long after his allotted time, departed the scene an abject and pathetic reject, the victim of ill-considered philanthropy.

'Never go against the tide boy,' Pius Mickelow had warned his brother Patcheen at the time. From the opposite side of the hearth Patcheen had nodded emphatically in total agreement.

Then came a particularly bitter winter of ice and snow and great sweeping gales, a winter that imposed a heavier than usual levy on the vulnerable and the elderly. The twins would remind each other that such winters were to be expected from time to time, winters that gave no quarter and for some, winters against which there was no defence.

Several old folk would pass on before the snows melted on the more elevated hilltops. Among these was a neighbour of the Mickelows, an eighty-five year old cottier and widower, one Daniel Doody, who had been nursed throughout the final weeks of his illness by his forty-five year old daughter who had given up her position as a domestic in the distant city of Cork and come home to attend to her ailing parent.

He bore his suffering bravely and all were agreed that his only offspring Kitty was truly a ministering angel if ever there was one.

Night and day she cared for him, luring him to upright positions on what would eventually be his deathbed with tit-bits and delicacies which had been prepared with love and devotion.

When, eventually, he expired, holding her hand, the hearts of the entire countryside went out to her but none more so than those of the twins Mickelow who had kept themselves discreetly at hand at all times when the old man strove to hang on forever to that which had been no more than a brief loan in the first place.

Patcheen Mickelow, in particular, was frequently moved beyond words as Kitty Doody tiptoed quietly to and fro uncomplainingly. Never once did she make

139

mention of her position in the city of Cork or of her lifestyle there. Rumour had it that she had once been friendly with a soldier but that he had left her for another after several fruitless years of courtship. Others had it that she had been a cook in a convent before leaving to take up a housekeeping post with an elderly schoolmaster. Still more maintained that she had worked as a drudge in an establishment of disrepute. There were other more fanciful tales but, as with all such idle speculation, another topic would displace it in no time at all.

Shortly after the moment of expiry on the fateful night Kitty Doody, her blue eyes filled with anguish, looked helplessly at the Mickelow twins who had been in close attendance all night. She had summoned them that evening in the realisation that the old man was nearing his end. He had been anointed the day before by Canon Mulgrave. The elderly cleric had advised Kitty Doody that she should be prepared for the worst and in consolatory tones assured her that her father would surely see heaven. A last feeble cry followed by a low choking sound heralded his passing.

'I'll go for the priest,' Patcheen Mickelow had announced with fitting solemnity.

'And I'll go for the neighbours,' Pius Mickelow had volunteered.

During the wake which followed, in the absence of relatives, the twins Mickelow acted as chief stewards and masters of ceremonies. It was they who distributed the wine, whiskey and stout and it was they who polished and shone the holders for the death candles. It was they who replenished the traditional saucers of snuff on mantelpiece, table and cranny all though the long night and morning.

During the wake Pius Mickelow drank his fill but never allowed himself to cross the threshold of drunkenness. For his part Patcheen allowed not a tint of liquor to pass his lips.

Afterwards when the whole business was at an end

Patcheen would partake of a drink or two but for the duration of the wake proper and while it was in progress he resolved that he would be the most responsible man at that wake. Of the twins he was by far the more resolute. It was he who decided that the town should be out of bounds after Pius was struck on the jaw one night many years before with a dustered fist for no reason whatsoever. The blackguards he encountered in the gents toilet had never seen him before nor had he seen them. Patcheen quite properly deduced that the only reasons why his twin was felled were his small statute and inoffensive manner. His pockets had not been rifled and he had not spoken a word.

'He is the sort,' Patcheen confided to the publican in whose premises the assault had taken place, 'who draws trouble on himself because of the way God made him.' He counted himself lucky to have escaped similar treatment himself at the hands of the many drunken blackguards who pack-hunted in large towns after dark.

Pius had agreed instantly when Patcheen suggested that they stick thereafter to familiar haunts where they were known and respected.

After the burial of Daniel Doody the Mickelows decided that they would not present themselves at the Doody household until such time as they were invited. Fine, they felt, to have made themselves available during the latter stages of the old man's illness but it would not be altogether appropriate to do so now without good reason.

Spring would be well advanced with the wild daffodils withdrawn and brown before such an invitation would be extended. In between they occasionally met Kitty on the roadway and they nodded respectfully towards each other after Mass on Sundays. Sometimes there would be words but these, for the most part, would be confined to views about the weather although Patcheen suspected that a more protracted exchange might not be unwelcome as far as Kitty Doody was concerned. For all that he played his cards in the conventional way and felt himself well rewarded when the invitation came on the final day of April. Pius was mightily pleased in his own way although the twins knew full well that the reason behind the summons was most likely related to the cutting and harvesting of the turf supply for the winter ahead.

For some years before his death as infirmity rendered him less active they had been hired by the late Daniel Doody to cut, foot and draw home the dry crop in their ancient but still serviceable ass-rail.

The drawing home was usually accomplished in less than a week and at the end of that time Daniel Doody's turf shed would be full to the rafters.

When they arrived at the Doody house they were made welcome at the doorway by the sole occupant, the beaming Kitty who took note of their sheepishness by seating them near the hearth and handing each a freshly-opened bottle of stout.

The Mickelows were pleased to learn that it was fresh and in prime condition. They would have been just as pleased to accept stout left over from the wake but this, they would be at pains to explain, was not Kitty's way at all.

She sat herself by the large, wooden table while the visitors drew on their bottles. They spoke about many matters. Every subject, in fact, was up for discussion save the one which brought them. That would be aired in its own time. It would have been a blatant breach of good manners to bring it up prematurely.

When a second bottle of stout and all the conventional topics had been exhausted Kitty Doody spoke for the first time about turf.

'I was wondering,' she said as her sad blue eyes swept the kitchen and finally the hearth-place where the twins were seated, 'what I should do about the winter's firing?'

'Turf is it you're worried about?' It was Patcheen who spoke on behalf of the pair.

142

'Turf it is,' Kitty Doody confirmed.

'Let turf be the least of your worries,' Patcheen Mickelow assured her.

'The very least of your worries,' his brother Pius added lest there be the slightest doubt about it.

'Her turf will be cut won't it boy?' Patcheen turned to Pius knowing full well what the answer would be. They had discussed the subject often enough across the winter nights.

'Let some one else try to cut it,' Pius had whispered to himself with uncharacteristic ferocity. Now the words gushed forth like a torrent as he pledged his commitment.

'We will first clean the turf-bank of scraws,' he said, 'and then we will cut it and foot it and refoot it and then we will make it up into donkey stoolins and then come September when it will be well seasoned we will fill your shed to the rafters.'

'That is exactly what we will do,' Patcheen concurred proudly. He was about to add further reassurances of his own but Pius had not yet finished.

'We will not be charging you a brown penny,' he rushed out the words lest he suddenly dry up, 'for we would be poor neighbours if we did not help a lady in a pucker.'

'Oh we can't have that,' Kitty Doody tried not to sound half-hearted, 'we can't have that at all. The labourer is worthy of his hire.'

'Not these labourers!' Patcheen cut across, 'these labourers is doing it out of the goodness of their hearts so there will be no more talk about hire.'

Relieved that her predicament had been shouldered by such a doughty pair she rose from the table and wiped a tear from her eyes with a corner of her apron. Her visitors had the good grace to turn their heads and used the opportunity to carefully examine the glinting soot which adorned the back wall of the chimney.

'If ye will come to the table now,' Kitty suggested

143

without the least sign of stress or worry in her voice, 'I will grease the griddle and we'll have fresh pancakes for supper.'

After that April visit the twins called regularly across the summer to render a progress report on their turf-cutting activities. Always there would be fresh pancakes and then one glorious day in the middle of June she made her way to the bog in order to see for herself the advances being made and to invite her champions home for supper.

The sun shone from a cloudless sky and from every quarter of the boglands the larks sang loudly especially when the sun departed the centre of the heavens and moved slowly down the sky.

'On such a day as this,' Patcheen Mickelow spoke with awe in his tone, 'God do give his voice to the larks and then the larks do tell us about God.'

'Oh well spoke brother, well spoke!' Pius made the sign of the cross reverentially and turned to Kitty whose sparkling blue eyes radiated appreciation of the heavenly sentiments expressed by Patcheen.

'Was it not well spoke Kitty?' Pius asked and then he fell silent as he awaited Kitty's reaction.

'It was well spoke,' Kitty Doody agreed, 'in fact it could not be better spoke if it was spoke about forever.'

Pius marvelled at the wisdom of her answer. For some time he had the feeling that the pair had a special relationship, nothing that he could put his finger on except that he knew it to be there.

'It's there,' he said to himself, 'as sure as there's frogs in the bog-pools and hares in the heather.'

'Oh you may say it was well spoke,' Kitty turned the full force of her blue eyes on Patcheen Mickelow but he could no more look directly into their depths than he could at the blazing sun which adorned the heavens. Modestly he bent his tousled grey head and sought refuge in the heather. Pius now knew for certain that there were exciting stirrings in the hearts

144

that beat close by and that when the stirrings co-mingled there would be a rare song in the air.

'Wouldn't it be lovely,' Kitty Doody whispered the hope half to herself, half to the twins, 'if this day could go on forever.'

The brothers were immediately arrested by the sentiment, impractical though it might sound.

'Yes, yes,' they whispered fervently, 'it would be lovely.'

For the remainder of the day Kitty helped with the making and clamping of the donkey stoolins and it was not she who cried halt as the shadows lengthened.

'If I don't eat soon,' Patcheen announced, 'my belly will never again converse with my gob.'

Taking each by an arm Kitty led them to a spongy passageway and thence to the dirt road which would take then to her home.

The summer passed uneventfully thereafter and then came the time for the drawing home of the turf. They made light work of the task and by the end of the second week in September the Doody shed was filled to capacity as promised. The turf was of the highest quality and properly utilised would keep the winter cold firmly in its place.

As usual the twins paid their bi-weekly visit to the pub at the crossroads and it was here one night that they overheard strange tidings which alarmed them to no end.

'She'll pine for the ways of the city, you'll see,' a local farmer informed another, 'and it's my guess,' he continued, unaware that he had an interested audience only a few yards away, 'that she'll make tracks as soon as her year's mourning is down.'

'What makes you say that?' the second farmer asked.

'I say that,' said the first farmer, 'because she has stopped wearing the black at Mass and when women stops wearing the black they gets anxious about the future and then they're likely to pull up stakes and to move or to marry as the humour catches them.'

That very night at the request of Pius the twins departed the pub after the second pint.

'Follow me,' he had said, 'and don't ask no questions like a good man.'

Although slightly irritated Patcheen was curious. Silently he followed his twin into the night. Despite his best efforts he found himself unable to draw abreast of his brother. He wanted to ask why they were making a detour and why he had been obliged to forego half of his normal intake but could not catch up so determined was Pius to reach his goal.

Eventually they found themselves at the gate which opened on to the Doody laneway.

'It's up to you now boy,' Pius confronted his brother, 'you better go in there and state your case or we might never see her again.'

'Look at the hour of the night we have!' Patcheen argued.

''Tis the right hour for what you have to do,' Pius insisted, 'and isn't there a light in the kitchen window which means she's still up.'

Patcheen Mickelow hesitated. If he was to tell the absolute truth he would admit to having considered the precise manoeuvre on which his brother wished him to embark on many an occasion but implementing it was another matter altogether.

'I won't know how to put it,' he complained.

'It will all come to you when you face up to her,' Pius assured him as he pushed him towards the gateway. At that moment the door opened and Kitty Doody appeared.

'Who's out there?' she called.

'It's only us,' Pius Mickelow returned.

'I'm so relieved,' Kitty called back as she placed a shaking hand under her throat. The brothers stood silently side by side, Pius nudging Patcheen to give an account of himself and the latter temporarily tonguetied.

146

'Is there anything wrong?' Kitty Doody asked anxiously after she had advanced a few paces.

'This poor man has something wrong with him all right,' Pius pushed Patcheen forward, 'but he'll be telling you all about it himself for I would say that it's been playing on his mind for some time.'

'Oh dear!' came the sympathetic response, 'there is none of God's creatures without some kind of a cross.' So saying she bent her head meekly and went indoors, making sure as she did that the door remained ajar behind her. At the same moment Pius Mickelow turned on his heel and disappeared into the night.

'Sit up to the fire,' Kitty removed a bundle of knitting from a chair near the hearth and sat herself on a chair nearby, nearer his chair Patcheen noticed than she had ever ventured before. His heart soared but then it flopped awkwardly downward into its rightful resting place when he considered the unpredictable ways of the opposite sex.

So far as Patcheen knew, and it was also believed by other eminent authorities, members of the opposite sex for reasons best known to themselves did not always make themselves quite clear in matters of the heart.

Faced with this dilemma he bided his time. Caution was called for and he would be the first to admit that he had no experience in dealing with women.

So profound was the silence in the kitchen, apart from the ticking of the mantelpiece clock, that the only sound to be heard came from the gentle criss-crossing of the knitting needles which Patcheen had never before seen so speedily and skilfully employed. Thus they sat for what seemed ages. From time to time he adjusted himself on the chair but there was no move from his companion saving the bewildering complexities of the knitting fingers. As far as he could see she seemed to be in a jovial mood. However, limited and all as his experience was, he knew that females often tended to make their meaning clear too late in the day with disastrous consequences.

Occasionally she would lift the blue eyes from her work and smile at him as if it was the most natural thing in the world that the two of them should be sitting together.

Then surprisingly she moved her chair nearer to his, so near that their bodies brushed whenever they adjusted themselves. It was a hopeful sign surely but she gave no other and as the night wore on it seemed that she might not move till dawn brightened the landscape beyond the curtained window.

'Unless I make a move now,' Patcheen told himself, 'I will never make one.'

'Do you know what I'm thinking?' he whispered confidentially.

'No,' came the conspiratorial reply.

'I was thinking,' said he, 'of what a waste it is to see two fires in two different houses when you could have just one fire in one house.'

'I know what you mean indeed,' she agreed, 'for it was often the same thought occurred to myself.'

'Waste not,' Patcheen recalled the first half of the ancient maxim.

'Want not!' she concluded it for him.

'Then there's the upkeep of the two houses,' he pressed his advantage. She nodded eagerly in accord.

'There's no telling the advantages,' he went on, at which she laughed and so did he.

'One of the houses would have to go,' she said.

'You mean for pour oul' Pius to stay here with us then?' he asked, hardly daring to believe his ears.

'We couldn't very well leave the poor creature on his own,' she replied, 'and isn't there a room to spare. We would have our room and he would have his, that's if he'll agree!'

'Oh he'll agree,' Patcheen assured her, 'there's nothing he'd like better.'

'That's good to hear,' she laid the knitting aside.

'All Pius ever wanted from the day he met you,'

Patcheen informed her, 'was to see the two of us settled. He worries that you may go off and leave us and never come back.'

'I won't be leaving,' she whispered as she turned the devastatingly blue eyes upward and in so doing presented her pursed lips for approval. Only a man of iron would have by-passed such an opportunity. Kiss her he did, not once but several times and not just on the lips but all over her face and her throat and her nose and her nape and her ears. It was the blue eyes that he wondered at most of all. They seemed never to be without a sparkle and they were filled too with wonder or so it seemed every time he gazed into them.

When they had kissed their fill she laid the table for tea. They drank cup after cup and spoke for hours. Canon Mulgrave would have to be consulted. They both knew that he would approve for was he not night and day vociferating his views about the absolute necessity for more marriages in the seriously depopulated parish and while discriminating pundits might argue that Kitty Doody was past it, others would counter by insisting that where there was life there was hope.

As things turned out there would be no issue but otherwise it was as happy a marriage as one could find in the parish or the many parishes beyond. As for the arrangement with Pius; he treated his sister-in-law with the utmost respect and was at pains at all times to show her that he knew his place and could be trusted beyond words.

Certain of their immediate neighbours who believed themselves to be possessed of rare powers of prognostication let it be known that it was their belief that the bi-weekly visits to the crossroads pub and to other harmless activities would be seriously curtailed when the twins moved into the Doody homestead. They were to be proved totally wrong.

As always the pair showed up at the crossroads and they were to be seen at football matches and coursing meetings in the many enterprising townlands and villages which hosted such events in their seasons.

It was noted too by interested parties who had made close studies of the affairs of others on the grounds that it was beneficial to the community as a whole that the twins looked better, were sprightlier of step and were never without the price of a drink in their pockets.

Time passed and the old ways of the countryside began to undergo changes. Donkey and carts began to disappear from the roadways and the bog passages. Tractors and trailers began to replace them.

Small, serviceable motor-cars replaced the horse and pony carts and the family traps as a means of transport to Mass and to village and occasionally to the town in the far away valley.

The twins Mickelow kept to the old ways for as long as was practicable but eventually after years of subtle prompting from Kitty, submitted to the new craze and invested in a venerable Morris Minor which both brothers learned to drive.

From a financial point of view they were never as well off so that the belated purchase of the car did not leave them in debt. All three had reached pensionable age before eventually deciding to invest in the Morris.

All around, other exciting changes were taking place in the villages and towns throughout the countryside. The old, musty, male-dominated public houses were being reconstructed and glamorous lounge bars began to replace them.

The crossroads pub, frequented by the twins, was among the last to conform to the modern style and the first female to accompany her men on a crossroads excursion on a Sunday night was the brave Kitty, wife of Patcheen Mickelow. In no time at all other females followed suit.

In short order came singalongs and dance music and even the clergy, for once, somewhat confused by the transition, kept their opinions to themselves and allowed the parish free rein in its appetite for modern entertainment.

The twins, lookalike as ever, grew frailer but retained both their rude health and appetite for enjoyment. Their tousled heads whitened in the face of the advancing years but their capacity for consuming stout declined not at all. Kitty kept the white and the grey at bay with various tints and lotions. The happiness the trio enjoyed from the day Patcheen married had mellowed into a pleasant contentment. Whatever the neighbours might opine they could never say that the Mickelows were poorly off. When the three old age pensions were tallied they realised a considerable income.

Then, alas, Kitty took ill and after a short illness passed away. The twins very nearly succumbed to the grief which followed. In the course of time the sorrow would be assuaged a little but they might never have visited the crossroads pub again had it not been for what Pius would later term, heavenly intervention.

It transpired that shortly before Kitty died she summoned Patcheen to their bedroom. She bade him be seated on the sole plush-covered chair which, up until this moment, had never been used to fill the role for which it had been designed. Coats, blouses, trousers and other articles of clothing had been draped across its back or dumped on the seat but it had never, in the course of its existence, been sat upon. It had none of the sturdiness of the kitchen chairs, was frail and rickety but was, after all, ornamental.

Patcheen sat awkwardly and listened intently to his wife's carefully prepared recital. She wished to be buried in the same grave as her late parents and she made him promise that when his time came for leaving the world he would join her there and Pius too if he so wished. He assured her that it would be their dearest wish. She next handed him a slip of paper with instructions for the smooth administration of her wake and funeral. On it was meticulously pencilled all that would be required in the line of drink and edibles. A silence followed. It was as though the business of briefing him had exhausted her. After a long pause she informed him that it was her wish to be laid out in her navy blue costume and white silk blouse.

'In the drawer over yonder,' she pointed weakly in the direction of the dressing table, 'you will find a blue ribbon to bind my hair.' Patcheen nodded. Her wish would be carried out were the heavens to fall.

'In the bottom drawer,' she continued hoarsely, 'you will find two envelopes. In one which is marked wake money you will find sufficient to cover the cost of my wake and funeral and in the other which is addressed to Canon Mulgrave is the money to pay for the special Masses for the repose of my soul and all the poor souls wherever they may be.'

During the long spring and summer which followed, the twins kept to themselves and were seen abroad only when they shopped at the crossroads or attended Mass.

Despite the provision made by Kitty they found themselves in debt. Instead of the modest oak coffin for which she had allowed in her calculations they opted for the most expensive walnut with the most ornate trappings.

They found themselves faced with two choices; to sell the Morris Minor or abstain from intoxicating drink until the undertaker was paid. In the space of a year according to Pius's reckoning they should be free of debt and also free to resume their visits to the crossroads pub. Then came the heavenly intervention referred to by Pius.

It so happened that after the Funeral Mass when Patcheen Mickelow approached Canon Mulgrave to pay for the Funeral Mass the Canon had expressed reluctance in accepting the extra money for the Masses which would be said for Kitty and the poor souls.

'Now, now,' Canon Mulgrave said, 'there's no need

at all for that. You've paid for the High Mass and that in itself is sufficient.'

Patcheen would have none of it. Mindful of his wife's clearly expressed instructions he forced the envelope upon the Canon and hurried from the scene.

Later that afternoon when the Canon opened the envelope he was surprised at the amount therein. Normally he would have been gratified if a pound or two had been forthcoming but he was truly astonished when he beheld the neatly folded twenty pound note. His conscience dictated that the money would have to be returned with the suggestion that a pound or two would do nicely in its stead. He knew for a certainty that the twenty pound note was far and away beyond the means of the twins. He resolved to return the note intact at the earliest opportunity. Some time would pass before he did. He would agonise every time he looked inside the envelope which he kept atop the mahogany desk in his study. He dithered for several months. There were times when he told himself that the money had been given with a good heart and there were other times when he tried to convince himself that it would be against the spirit of the dead woman's intent if he did not accept the money. He decided that the Masses should be celebrated without more ado and he also decided that further cogitation would be required before he finally decided on the destination of the twenty pound note.

It turned out that shortly before Christmas the Canon's letter box was flooded by a deluge of neglected bills. He withdrew the twenty pound note from its envelope. With infinite care he smoothed it on top of his desk. It would go a long way towards discharging his debts. Then he manfully reminded himself that the Christmas dues would shortly commence to replenish the presbytery coffers. This left him with only one choice. The twenty pound note would have to be returned.

He chided himself for his long-term tardiness and

lack of Christian resolution. He sat in his car and drove to the abode of the Mickelows. Pius it was who greeted him at the door. The Canon gracefully declined the invitation to enter.

The Canon, like all the canons and curates before him, had long since given up the impossible task of telling the twins apart. However, as far as this particular mission was concerned, one twin was as good as the other.

Earlier that morning Patcheen had set out for a distant grove where he would cull a sufficiency of holly and ivy to decorate the crib and the kitchen.

'Now my dear man,' Canon Mulgrave held the twenty pound note aloft, 'I must tell you that this note you see before you is rightfully yours. It was far too much and I am conscience bound to return it.'

Mystified, Pius Mickelow gazed with open mouth at the money and when he had gazed his fill he gazed secondly at his visitor. When the Canon thrust the twenty pound note into the gnarled hand Pius Mickelow decided to play along although his mystification had greatly increased and he was now convinced beyond reasonable doubt that the Canon had succumbed to the dotage which few escape at the end of their days.

'Not a word now sir!' the Canon raised an admonishing finger, 'not a word no matter what. This is strictly between you and I. The Masses have been said so you can set your mind at rest. The money is yours to do with as you please. I'll be on my way now and I sincerely hope that you and your brother enjoy a happy and a holy Christmas.'

The Canon would relish the forthcoming Christmas. His conscience had been salved. He had acted as a true Christian.

On the Sunday evening before Christmas the twins sat at either side of the hearth. They had sat for over an hour without exchanging a word. It was Pius who broke the silence.

'What say we go to the pub,' he suggested matter of factly. Thinking that he had not heard aright Patcheen inclined his head.

'What's that you say?' he asked.

'The pub,' Pius threw back.

'And what will we use for money?' Patcheen asked sarcastically. Pius produced the twenty pound note for the first time.

'Is it real?' Patcheen asked as he took the note in his hand. Satisfied that it was the genuine article he asked where it came from.

'I am not at liberty to say,' Pius answered solemnly, 'but it wasn't found and it wasn't stolen. The man who gave it to me made me promise that I would never tell.'

'Lets move,' Patcheen rose and donned his overcoat. Pius followed suit.

'And you can't say where it came from?'

'Can't say,' came the reply, 'but this I will say, 'it came from God through man and if it came from God you may be sure that Kitty had a hand in it.'

SPREADING JOY
AND JAM AT
CHRISTMAS

LET HIM WHO can boast of no failing take a bow for he is a unique fellow. He is elite among the elite but I would not have his impeccable status for all the lamb on Carrigtwohill.

Carpers will ask why I open on such a vein, what arrant nonsense am I proposing to inflict upon them as winter deepens and Christmas draws near.

I am actually about to recall an outing which took place a week before Christmas, at a time when my hair was black and you'd get a pint for two bob. The hero of the piece is no longer with us but if ever a man was cut out to play Santa Clause, he was that man. He could, in fact, fill any role.

It is many years now since this Mayo friend of mine and I set out for his native county where we proposed to spend a few days carousing and visiting the friends of his boyhood.

As we left Tubbercurry one evening shortly before Christmas on our way into Mayo he recalled the school where he had spent, according to himself, a wasted youth.

His teacher had been a grumpy fellow who regarded my friend and most of the other pupils as irredeemable illiterates and he would warn them day after day that they would never be fit for anything but the most menial of tasks.

'O'Donnell,' he would say to my friend, 'all I want is to see you able to spell for when you go to England your people won't know where you are because you won't be able to write and tell them.'

Actually O'Donnell was able to read and write before ever he went to the national school but he realised that if this fact became known he would find himself out on a limb. His illiterate companions might have no more to do with him. Better, he felt, be a fool among other fools than a star whose brilliance might be his undoing.

When we arrived in Claremorris we stopped at a well-known hostelry. Outside the door we noticed a large van full of jam. There were crates of one pound and two pound pots from floor to ceiling. There was raspberry, strawberry and plum. There was gooseberry, marmalade and mixed fruit.

'It's a terror,' said my friend, 'to see so much jam exposed to the naked eye and half the world starving.' He shook his head at the injustice of it.

In the bar we treated ourselves to two amber deorums of Irish whiskey and while were sipping from same a young girl entered and approached my friend.

She had somehow mistaken him for the driver of the jam van. In fact he could be mistaken for anybody. He had that kind of face. A woman once gave him a pound to say Mass. He had been wearing a dark suit on the occasion.

'Sir,' said the young girl, 'my mother wants to know would you have any cracked pot? Strawberry or marmalade or mixed fruit or anything at all will do.'

'Musha what do you want a cracked pot for?' my friend asked, 'and the van loaded with sound pots.'

'Can I have a pot so sir, a one-pound will do?'

'And has your mother a conveyance?' my friend asked.

'Oh she has sir,' said the girl. 'She has an ass and car.'

'Tell her to load a few crates,' said my friend, 'but not to overdo it. Ye don't want to make pigs of yeerselves entirely.'

'Oh no sir,' said the girl and she ran from the bar,

a transformed creature.

Shortly afterwards we left the pub and proceeded to our car which we had parked nearby.

There was no sign of the jam van.

We walked through the town and a delightful walk it was. I would recommend a walk through Claremorris for any and all persons down in the dumps. The friendliness of the people was matched by the cleanliness of the streets and the disposition of the town as a whole.

There were some who came forward and shook our hands, tendering to us the most profuse welcomes to Mayo and the town itself.

One old woman complained of dizzy spells when we enquired after her health. My friend took her pulse and asked if she was taking anything for her complaint. She recalled visits to several doctors and reeled off a long list of medicines. None had done her any good. She seemed to be growing worse rather than better. My friend shook his head as he listened.

'Do you take a lot of spring water?' he asked after he had heard all he wanted to hear.

'Only in tea,' she said, 'and mostly from the tap.'

'Drink plenty spring water,' he advised. 'Spring water never did anybody any harm.'

The old woman nodded eagerly.

'Eat plenty vegetables,' he went on, 'especially cabbage and take a drop of the hot stuff morning and night.'

'I declare to God and His blessed Mother,' said she, 'but I feel better already. It was God sent you this way. I'll pray for you.'

'Pray for us all,' said my friend and he strolled off in the direction of the mountains or more particularly in the direction of Ballyhaunis where he had a large number of relations from his mother's side. I was left holding the baby as it were.

'Is he a doctor?' the old woman asked.

'No,' I informed her, 'he's not a doctor.'

'A specialist then?' she asked hopefully.

'Yes,' I replied, 'he's a specialist.'

Of course he was a specialist, a specialist in cheering people up and a specialist in dispersing gloom.

Eventually we found ourselves driving out of town. A slight mist was drifting down.

In Mayo mists don't fall down. They drift down. We drove slowly. There was no need for words between myself and this natural dispenser of goodness.

'Glory be to God!' he exclaimed when we beheld an ass and cart on the left hand side of the road. At each side of the body sat a female. One was shawled and old. The other was young and beautiful. Their faces were radiant with happiness and contentment.

In the cart were two cases of jam; one was filled with one pound pots and the other with two pound pots. He lowered the window of the car and saluted the pair. The girl waved at him ecstatically. Turning to me he said: 'Were we to depart life now we would surely see heaven for the happiness we spread this day.'

Glossary

Bodhrán – one-sided, goat-skin drum
Cadhrawn – small sod of peat
Cob – horse
Cronawning – purring or buzzing
Crubín – pig's feet
Cúram – responsibility (family)
Deorum – drop, from the Irish *deor*, a tear
Didlers – singer of words without music
Frost-nails – special nails for horses' hooves in frost
Garsún – young boy
Groodle – additive to soup
Jowl – neck of bottle
Lorgadawn – leprechaun
Oat's money – money to buy oats for priests' horses
Pillalooing – demented crying
Reek – heap of turf neatly clamped
Scraws – grass-covered sod of earth or peat top-sod
Stoolin – heap of dried peat
Sugán – straw-woven chair